I0598705

# IF WE
# WERE ONE

Dave Haywood

Fisher King Publishing

IF WE WERE ONE

Published by
Fisher King Publishing

fisherkingpublishing.co.uk

For my readers...

Thank you to you all. Past, present, and future. Without you, these stories would go forever unheard.

And of course to the legendary emergency services risking their lives all around the world.

To Dad, I miss you. I am still trying. Mum is bossing it, so don't worry. But mainly, and always, still for Rebecca and Riley.

## Introduction and Acknowledgements

Hopefully, you are here because you read 'What We Leave Behind' or dipped your toe into the new world of 'The Darktouched' and didn't leave it behind in the shop. (Something tells me you will after reading this though... hint hint) It's fine if you are a new reader, as all are always welcome. You are my lifeblood after all! There may be spoilers in this book for 'What We Leave Behind' though, so you have been warned... Who am I kidding? There are massive ding dong ones.

So, book two in the 'Humanity Falls' series... It's lovely getting this one out of my head as it's taking up book three space! That ones called 'Bloodlines' by the way. What I have planned for that one will knock any socks you have left on, clear off.... I have tried to keep these books as standalone as possible, but if you read them in order, you'll get some backstory and hints/secrets of what's to come in the overall arc. Did you catch them in 'What We Leave Behind'? It may be worth a reread before this rollercoaster... Go buy it if you haven't already and read that one first! (Please, thank you! You're amazing.)

I am also working on a palette cleanser to the psychological thriller stuff in the working title of 'The Darktouched,' which is a Fantasy Romantasy style fantasy thriller... Let's see how that one goes... (Author's note, it may already be out as I've been waiting for someone to sign this one off for ages.) (Author's second note. It is.)

For those that are still new to my books... Hi, I'm Dave, and I have dreamed of being an author for as long as I can remember. At sixteen, I wrote a novella called 'The Soul of the Gem' and I sent it to Headline Publishing who sent a lovely postcard back saying how much they liked it, and that if I made some changes, it might be a thing! Life then left-turned and I never followed that advice. Stupid Dave. But now I'm an official author and get to say thank you to all the wonderful people who helped me through everything I have faced.

As always, firstly to my family and mainly my mum. She's been a stalwart supporter of everything I do and has made me who I am today. She even bought me a mug with my first book cover on it. It's not been an easy road in recent years though, as I lost my dad abruptly just before my first book came out, so my writing stopped for a while so I could look after Mum. But even through it all, she still found the strength to say 'My son's an author' to everyone we passed. With that courage, I'll continue to try and make her proud, and if I haven't already, I'll just keep trying.

Then there's Shreen. My lovely wife. Seeing her face after she finished 'What We Leave Behind' will stay with me forever. She was so proud. I love that about her. She's been awesome through this all, but is really fed up now of 'Pirate Otter Adventure' songs. Which, in all honesty, is fair enough. Heave ho.

I want to thank my gaming group, the Heroes and Halfwits who all bought the first one and then made me sign them. May we continue into that dark night with Ellycea stressfully trying to keep Daiki, the Dragonborn tank, at full health. (Author's note, we moved on to "Curse of Strahd so I'm now a high half elf called Lanyariss. He's a bit of a dick.)

Fisher King should also get a mention here as without them, I'd never be here. They had enough faith in 'What We Leave Behind' to bring 'If We Were One' to life. I will always be appreciative of them for making me an official author. Thanks, Rick, Sam, and Rachel, you utter legends...

Again, to my team of beta / ARC readers who kept me going and picked me up. You are truly amazing.

I'd also like to thank the team at the #BookParty for arranging an event where I could speak to readers and meet other authors. All were massive in comparison to me, but so, so lovely. John Marrs, Suzie Edge, A.J. West, L.V. Matthews, T.M. Logan, Jackie Kabler, Janice Hallet, Sam Holland, and Tom Mead were all competing for the nicest author alive.

And then there's Kaleigh Cancetty BA(Hons). My hard taskmaster. My editor. My proofreader. My champion. You helped me get the book into the world, and I'll never forget your 5 STAR REVIEW! (She's helped replace the word boobies, among a host of other things).

And lastly, thank you to all you readers and followers who have supported me on this wild journey. I hope you like this second book as much as the others. It's all for you at the end of the day.

⅄ Instagrammers - Kim, Leigh, Jessi, Becky, Sarah, Tyronne, Jade, Emily, Louise, and Linzie. (And another Stacy, but she's more on Tiktok).

⅄ The Bound by Books club - Stacey, Eilidh, Scott, Amanda, Sophie, Rae, Tammy, Laura, Jade, Sadie, Dannie and Chloe.

⅄ Authors - Phoebe, Russell, Oliver, Traci and Sara.

⅄ And a special shoutout to Mikko. Woof. Good doggo.

Thank you for pushing this little guy.

Brace yourself.

Here we go.

Again.

## Prologue One

It was at that moment, that briefest of seconds, that I felt my life end.

## Prologue Two

There are two sides to every coin.

Yin always has its yang.

Reactions to actions.

And when it comes down to it, brass tacks and all, Good versus Evil.

Throughout time the two warring factions have sparred, trying desperately to get one foot higher than the other. Stepping on their backs, they fought for supremacy. Both sides would employ different tactics and contrasting voices, from angered feelings to thoughtful emotions, from insidious actions to feral motives. But both aimed for a similar destiny. Always trying to outwit. To crush the other. To win. Over the years, some of these battles became internal struggles, hidden deep within or out bursting forth. Wars raged without sight, existing in pure emotion versus the controlled serenity peace brought. Chaos and anarchy could never win over total control though, so a perpetual balance would always succeed but  always be uneasy.

This war continued to rage in silence, screaming in stillness. In this unseen desolate landscape, the two warring factions continued to face each other, locked in a silent and eerie confrontation. The absence of gunfire and battle cries rendered the scene surreal as if the very air held its breath in anticipation, waiting for the first to break. Emotions on either side exchanged glares that spoke louder than any words could ever. A mixture of determination, weariness, and the weight of unspoken grievances and traumas

The war-weary combatants moved with a ghostly quietness, their movements calculated and deliberate, as if acknowledging the gravity of the moment. Amidst the silence, the tension hung thick, and the absence of audible conflict only heightened the palpable animosity between the adversaries. In this strange symphony of stillness, the clash of ideologies and the muted struggle for dominance unfolded, leaving an indelible mark on the imaginary battleground where silence spoke louder than any war cry ever could.

There are no tanks, no soldiers, no spies.

There are no aircraft dog-fighting on dark, stormy nights.

Here, there is only emotion.

And it's packed.

### Breaking News: Tragedy Strikes Epsom, Surrey in Devastating Night of Violence

Epsom, Surrey – The quiet town of Epsom has been left in shock after a series of harrowing incidents overnight that have resulted in multiple deaths, leaving families devastated and the community reeling. Surrey Police are currently investigating what they describe as a 'deeply disturbing' sequence of events, with officers and emergency services working through the night to respond to the unfolding tragedy.

Details remain scarce at this stage, but it has been confirmed that several lives were lost in what police are calling 'grizzly and tragic circumstances.' The exact nature of the incidents has not yet been made public, but initial reports suggest that the impact has torn several families apart and left the town in mourning.

In an official statement, Superintendent Becky Douglas of Surrey Police expressed her profound sorrow at the devastation that has unfolded. "This is an unimaginable tragedy, and our thoughts are with the families and loved ones of those who have lost their lives in these horrific circumstances," she said. "We are working tirelessly to understand exactly what has happened and ensure that justice is served for those affected."

Local authorities have cordoned off several areas of Epsom, and a heightened police presence is expected in the coming days as investigations continue.

Residents are urged to remain vigilant and report anything suspicious as the situation develops.

Further updates are expected as more information becomes available.

As multiple crime scenes are in place throughout the area, please check your travel route for possible delays and diversions.

Sky News will continue to bring you the latest on this developing story.

The police had no further updates at this time.

# Chapter One

## Beginning and ending in 1993

The welcoming green gates were always open on a Friday night. They waited there for all the incoming parents to drop their most prize of possession at the various after-school clubs and activities Cheam School offered. There were a few choices, ranging from trampolining to drama. You could tell who was going to which club based on the outfits, as the more spangly they got, the more stories they told. Cars came and went. Various leotards ran through the car park on their way to the dance hall above the gym where the white Ford Escort was aiming for. The younger occupant had his head stuck deep within the pages of a Spiderman comic that warned of the coming invasion of the spider slayers ominously on the cover. Poor Mr Parker seemed to have gotten caught in his web which seemed ironic to the older man.

Amazing Spiderman three seven three was boldly proclaimed in the corner. Michael tried to limit his son's comic time but, being an avid reader himself, thought it was a little pot racistly bullying the kettle. He bought the comics for himself as much as his son and secretly loved the fact that he was into the same well-drawn content. The artwork evoked the very sense of the wind sweeping across Peter's latex red and blue suit giving an intense feeling of what the web-held flight must've felt like.

'Thankfully, we're both nerds for the Parker,' he thought, knowing that the artistry of Todd McFarlane, Mark Baggley, and John Romita, Sr. had brought the two geeks together even more than their bloodline normally would. Michael tried to be open and honest with his boy and it was rubbing off, with the younger one always owning up to the meagrest of dalliance. He loved his son with his all and seeing him, just sitting in a car, made the older man brim full of pride. He felt simply lucky. Bumping over a rather unforgiving speed hump alerted the boy that they were at their destination, and as the car drew to a stop, he said;

"You stay here Dad. I can walk in on my own." The young lad proclaimed with an authority above his years as they both got out of the car.

"Just because you can, doesn't mean you should..." came the response. The look of defiance was one pleading for trust as recently he'd been wanting more and more independence. This was something Michael was not, and would never be ready to give up fully, but he allowed it this time.

'What could go wrong right?' he concluded parentally. He had already weighed up the minimal risk. His boy was going to walk about thirty feet and then go into a door that led directly to the gymnasium of a school. Perfect. He could show trust in his son while not risking anything. A parenting win. The boy beamed as he turned, running to his trampoline club with his water bottle sloshing tightly in his grip. It knocked against a metal railing as he happily bolted to the gym door. Michael was left alone In the darkening school car park and pushed himself further into the driver's seat, trying to get as comfy as the hour wait would allow. He emptied his pockets for further comfort, unloading them onto the dashboard, and picking up the comic his son had dashed aside.

'He may love the story and the characters, but needs

to learn some paper-based respect.' Thought Michael as he settled into the prime reading position. He watched as parents filtered out of the car park for the hour of peace the classes offered and mulled over the idea of going home. But then he'd have to do chores and there'd be no spider-based action. So he decided to stay and began flicking through the pages of the comic he'd read already, taking in the artwork this time, rather than the lettering.

'Black cat was hot,' he thought and dreamed about being caught in a love triangle with the fur-clad vixen and the red-headed Mary Jane. Michael sighed and smiled warmly at the thought. Forty-five minutes slipped by and he realised that the light of the last day in June was dwindling.

There was just enough light left though to highlight the fleeting movement easily, not that he could tell what it was. He sat up, squinting through the windscreen, looking around for further signs of life in what he'd just seen. He'd only caught a glimpse of the grey fur over the top of the steering wheel, putting it down to a cat or a rat. The first option would most definitely need to be rubbed as the feline lover in him required. Not so much the second though, vile things.

Opening the car door he looked around the car park, which had a smattering of vehicles. One woman three cars down was reading a novel he couldn't make out, and she was paying no attention to anything else. Michael surmised it was either a book about a courtroom drama à la John Grisham or something more Mills and Boonie.

Again, movement off to his left.

Again, he didn't see it, just the sound of bare feet on asphalt. Hearing the padding crossed rat off the list, and upgraded it to fox or maybe a loose dog. Although the brief glimpse of grey fur earlier didn't help with identification.

He stood up, trying to get a better look, standing from the car. He left one foot inside and with one hand on the roof and one on the door, Michael felt like a ship's captain, looking out over the seven seas. The thought distracted him from the furred thing momentarily as he looked at his crew of swarthy imaginary sailors saying, "Yo Ho!" a little too much. He must have a word about their vocabulary, he noted. His body twitched a warning, bringing Captain Figment back to the shores of reality, so he flicked on the headlights of the car for a better look. Squinting at everything he could focus on, he tried to find the furtive source.

Nothing.

He turned the full beam into life trying to see what was scurrying about, but nothing was in the yellowed glow of the illuminated school car park.

Pat, pat, pat... More movement.

Michael turned his head as the large jaws clamped around his face from the grey-furred beast on the car roof. He was unable to scream, as the sickening crunch of his jawbone filled his ears.

## Chapter Two

One Monday in 2024…

### The Watcher

The outline of the person standing in the pitch-black room was only highlighted by the rising of the full moon. As it rose, it outlined the form perfectly, its brilliant light glancing off the toned body. Shoulders moved visually as each breath drawn was full-bodied and heavy. Each lungful of air was an outward display of emotion. The breath was vocal and intense, filled with excited anticipation. Sweat dripped down the tensed, muscular form. The droplets ran down the body, tracing the lines of sinew, a damp river journeying on a downward trek. The moonlight caught and glistened on the moist form, which was tensed and ready. It could move at any moment, such was the heightened state it was in.

Prepared and excited. It was again time to release the beast.

The raw emotional state called for its expulsion, screaming for it joyously. Excitement and trepidation built within its powerful frame. The light caught the dull white of teeth unclean as lips parted by the insane smile. It was not formed of happiness or joy, but of a manic hunger, needing to be satisfied.

The body quivered while the thrill built further as the incoming, yet challenging, outdoor pursuit grew nearer. They would be tested once more. But 'pursuit' was too timid a word.

To hunt. To capture. To kill.

The anticipation of heading out into the urban

wilderness, surrounded by the sights, the sounds, and the smells of city-born nature, always stirred a sense of excitement that was unmatched.

It could smell the hunt. It could smell everything. Taste the scent of the night to come. The odours drove the form wild and weren't masked by the intense sweating the form was undergoing. The sweating caused beads of moisture to glisten on their forehead and trickle down their temples. The smell that emanated from them was pungent, a combination of stale sweat mixed with hints of saltiness. It filled the air with an almost overpowering presence, leaving a lingering impression in the small bedroom. Their perspiration seemed to saturate the very atmosphere, creating an uncomfortable environment if anyone dared to enter. It couldn't be helped. It was the incoming pursuit's fault. Not even the hottest sex came close, although the same wild abandonment was similar in feeling. It left appendages tingling and sensitive to the touch.

The quiet moments before the kill of waiting, lurking in the darkness, or stalking through the concrete woodland were incredibly invigorating. The pursuit of game, whether for sport or sustenance, brought a profound connection to the primal instincts of bloodlined ancestors. The thrill of the hunt lay not in the possibility of success because that was certain with these cattle. It was in the heat of the blood. The tearing of flesh.

And the culling of the herd.

The time was now, and the beast was rising.

## Chapter Three

### Introducing Detective Sergeant Jack

I looked down at the immaculate desk. Beautiful. Moving my hands across the cleanliness of my workspace, I admitted to feeling a little proud that everything was in its correct and proper place. Even the matching pens in the pot stood level with each other, like decorated soldiers awaiting a major inspection, upright and true. The only thing amiss though, was that within the clear cases of the biros, they all had different black ink levels within their plastic bodies. Some even had air bubbles in and that was causing me some distress. It was as if they were all proclaiming their difference in effectiveness that I didn't want or ask for. Some of them weren't even trying.

Nope, can't.

I picked up the three pens and returned them to the stationary cupboard, which was stacked haphazardly. It's used by multiple teams of differing organisational abilities. You could clear it up one day and then a Tasmanian devil would whoosh through by the next, causing utter chaos. But fortunately, for now, the shelving contents were out of my desk's eyeline. Choosing four new pens, I returned to my seat, placing them in the correct holder. Better. But not perfect. So, I straightened them. Then turned them the other way up so that the ink would gravitationally fall nibwards, thus increasing effectiveness. This might all seem a bit much, but I've always been a bit of a stickler for order, which was handy in my line of work.

My name is Jack. Detective Sergeant Jack Wright to give me the full rank and title. I'd been running Surrey

Police's Criminal Investigation Department, or CID for those that love an acronym. I've been based in the idyllic, but busy, town of Epsom in the greenery of Surrey for a while now. I was head of team 4 and couldn't be prouder. They worked hard and helped to keep it both a lovely place to work and live. It was my life's main aim and it helped to keep things tight, so I would follow my strict and orderly code. It was something I always remember having as I'd always wanted to be a police officer from as early as I could remember. I was blessed with a longing for order over chaos and it became a driving force throughout my very existence.

Being so focused from such a young age did make me one of the weirder children though. In my parent's view, I mean. And, well, the teachers. Okay, and all the other kids. It might have been because I could never bring myself to be the 'robber' only ever the cop. When chasing my classmates around the school playground I would always insist upon their capture, and that all the correct processes my young mind knew of were followed. This was when they'd get bored, and play would dissolve as soon as the paperwork was produced from the small flip notebook I always carried. They'd then run off to play pat ball, British bulldog, or something less organised, leaving me with the custody filing.

'If you're going to do something, do it Wright.' I thought, beaming at the wild and chaotic use of my name replacement in the quotation. I could be a maverick at times. I joined the school council as a health and safety officer, which was my first official rank. Although it came with no uniform, just a badge that another pupil had made. The building blossomed as ten-year-old me allowed no deviations, and it made the venue an impregnable fortress of safety. It worked to outside eyes too as my primary school gained an 'outstanding' Ofsted report after I met the visiting inspectors and fully explained what the school's aims were. I'd taken the visit incredibly seriously to the point that my parents, and teachers, thought that I could have some special educational needs. My life continued its controlled route and to this point in early January 2024, I think I had barely faltered. Some cases did press against my chaos nerve, but I used science and logic to quash all irregularities, allowing finality for the victims. It was always the end goal to support the victims and it assisted in giving me one of the highest rates of case closure in any policing career. I am not bragging about it mind you. This is the job, and I am here to help.

One incident would always stick with me though. It completely changed my life. Thoughts of the terrible events come flooding back at the weirdest of moments. It makes me stop and reboot myself, as I cannot let the questions arise again. It's happening now, so I'll have to process and take stock of the incident one year ago. I'll never forget it, because certain inconsistencies plagued me still, even to this day. The deaths. The reflection in the shop mirror. The… well, everything.

My mood darkened as the evidence rose in my mind once again.

# Chapter Four

## 'What we leave behind'

### Jack

I leaned back in my chair as the recalled events played through in order. I tried to lay them out in statement form as best as I could. As best as my limited emotions allowed. A police officer had engaged with a member of the community and had a profound effect on the male's medical condition. The elderly person, who had hidden away a torrid and lengthy history of violence, was believed to have been suffering from the later stages of dementia and had not uttered a word to anyone in the care home he long resided in. It also transpired that he was into some extreme body modifications that only came to light after his death. This is something that has baffled everyone since. Even in the autopsy, the coroner was left with a terminal head scratch.

The PC… His name was Alex, had been murdered by the aforementioned elderly male after he killed a fellow resident and care worker shortly before Alex's arrival. CCTV from the venue had been a brutal watch. It is even shown to this day to officers to remind them that all situations you enter should be classed as 'unknown' as you do not know what people are capable of until they do it. Alex's murder was a hit to the borough, his team, and everyone. His superintendent had made sure he'd had a hero's funeral, with the blues and twos worthy of an officer who had died executing the course of his duties.

'Executing was the wrong phrase to use there,' I thought morbidly. The funeral was a thing of beauty though as everyone was decked out in their finest tunics. Horses wore their darkened caparison dress with solemn pride and the National Police Air Service flew overhead. Officers from across the service stood in silence as the traffic team cleared the streets, barely holding it together for the now thinner blue line.

There were no dry eyes. Even the more stoic of officers wept openly. It took weeks before anything close to normalcy returned, but policing always continued as criminals did not respect any sort of mourning period. The loss hung in the air still though. It made the offices, especially the safer neighbourhood team room feel very, very lonely. His team had all but disbanded as his work family could not bear to be around reminders of their fallen colleague. Sergeant McClaren had been Alex's skipper, and his death had been taken exceedingly hard by Jess. She transferred to response from neighbourhoods, to try and rebuild her career after the devastation. She had wanted to go as far as to move borough but had been convinced to stay by her inspector, as he did not want to lose another excellent officer.

'Having lost me already,' I think.

But to myself, the 'vulnerable' old man took away much of the grief. He was unexplained chaos. I could never truly know the reason for the modifications he'd made, or had been made to him. Or why he committed all those murders? Due diligence brought me to raise as many cold cases as I could link to Gerald which helped keep me focused. I had to eventually explain some of his actions to his deteriorating mental health and diagnosed dementia though. Something I was not happy with doing.

It seemed like almost an excuse for such horrendous actions.

Claire Chambers, Alex's wife, had also caused issues for the investigation. The coroner had ruled her death as inconclusive as there were no ligature marks of a noose, nor any bruise marks common with strangulation. The wounds all appeared internal at the time of examination, with bones in her neck not just broken, but pulverised, shattered beyond any human grip. Her windpipe also seemed to resemble a towel that had been wrung out, crushing any chance of receiving breath. Again, the coroner was at a loss, so he ruled it an impossibility to conclude murder.

After that, I put in for a transfer. The chaos was making me unfocused, as I constantly strived for the scientific reason behind it all. There simply wasn't one. I had to try to block these wild chaotic ideas as they did not fit with my sanity. My Inspector had begged me to stay, but I had my mind set on a new start away from the anarchy I had witnessed.

"How often have I said to you that when you have eliminated the impossible, whatever remains, however improbable, must be the truth?" Was the one Sherlock Holmes quote I couldn't abide by? Science was all, and he was the detecting master of it. My chair creaked underneath my leaning, not because of my weight though, as I had earned a runner's physique.

"You're all sinewy Jack!" My mother would say, trying to force-feed me lashings of roast dinner at my regular weekly visits. She meant well, but I enjoyed the athleticism I had worked hard for.

The next irregularity was the image in the reflection.

Even I was at a loss. So, I left it out of any reports as there was no crime or evidence that it could add. Christ only knows what the body-worn video had picked up. It was too much, and I needed order, so I snapped myself back into the room. Even now it haunts me.

Leaving my thoughts, I caught sight of the chaos of my new nemesis Detective Constable Gareth Derby's desk, and I visibly shuddered. It was merely feet away from my own. I thought that when I moved services, one of the benefits of the transfer was that I left Mike Granger, but it seems every office had 'that' employee. Gareth had his thoughts in the right place as Mike did, but his efforts were counting down the last few days till he retired. I did want to see the back of him though (professionally) as I wanted dynamic thinkers in team four, not poor-quality paper pushers trying to find any loopholes of ease.

When I joined Surrey I was already a sergeant, so transferred like for like, and one of my first jobs was to rearrange the office to place the skipper's desk in an area where it could see the entire workspace. Not in a 'view over your dominion' way though, more so that my team could speak to me from every angle, an unconscious open invite to my team. I've been told I can come across as robotic or even 'weird' as Elliot the school bully in primary school had often repeated, so this was my effort to be human. I was eager to be approachable and also supportive of my new team, borough and service, and it quickly earned me a name for being a decent skipper, one that an officer could talk to and know their back was covered. (Unless lines were crossed and then hell was truly to be paid).

'Look after your team and they'll do the Wright thing' I mused, happy with my eccentric use of my name once again. One thing that Alex's death had shown was that staff welfare was paramount. I made sure to check on people daily, but without being annoying.

Unconsciously though, the new desk arrangement was to move Gareth just that little bit further away. A happy bonus benefit. The clutter on his desk was like a virus and could easily spread to other connected areas if given the chance. I very much wanted not to catch anything chaotic. I'd even gone so far as to place strategic filing cabinets in eyelines. I realised that I was going too far when I considered bringing out the medical Perspex barriers to ward off the clutter and hem him in further.

The strident barking of the radio refocused my mind once again as my team was being called to assist with another response case. Initially assigned to it was my new transfer, Detective Constable Victoria Doherty, who'd joined three months ago. She beamed a request to be called 'Vikki' on her very first day. Her smile and boundless energy were infectious, quickly making her a staple on the team. Even I had allowed myself the dalliance with the frivolity of the abbreviation, although why she spelt it that way would forever be a mystery. Vicky, surely?

"Go team 4," I said out loud as I gathered the items needed for the call.

"I'll drive"

## Chapter Five

## Night Duty

### Jack

The streets of Epsom were alive at this time of night, due to the various clubs and bars all flashing their offers of enticement. Bouncers and doorstaff stood tall in their unofficial black hard-man outfits to dissuade any drunk entrants trying their luck, nodding as the various glittered dresses wobbled inside. January was a rough time, licensing-wise, with people stuffed and overspent from Christmas. Not only were the establishments competing for any leftover pounds, but they were also fighting the 'New Year, New You' brigade who, ironically, also wanted their clientele to lose pounds.

The unmarked Ford Focus was flashing blue lights, more as a warning for the drunk patrons wandering into my driving line, than to entice speed from the ageing vehicle. We wanted to be on scene as soon as we could, but safety first. I checked the overall details on the way down as Vikki and Detective Constable James Hills followed. We were en route to a suspected break-in, where the victim had been awoken from their slumber, by the 'crash tinkle' of glass. I chose to drive, so the investigating officers could prepare themselves for the task ahead. This left me to be there to support, supervise their professionalism, and help where needed. I'd hoped that due to the time of the call, the suspect would be in the area too, so we could nab us a 'William Burglar.'

DC Hills was scrolling through the details of the CAD, trying to stay as still as the blue light passenger seat trip would allow. He was pointing out the pertinent points to all the occupants.

"Night duty is on scene, with a second unit doing an area search, (currently no trace). The location is Old Barn Road, Epsom, and access to the property was probably gained through a side alley or wooded area. Houses are mainly semi-detached with some broken for rear access and garages. It's a lovely road, so maybe a chance opportunity for the suspect."

A slight chuckle at the words 'rear access' came from the back seat, as James continued his description. Tutting, he continued.

"No entry to the property, but the rear window was smashed, some minor damage to the frame. The occupant said that their dog might have scared off the intruder. No shed to access so wasn't for bikes. The garage was also untouched, so not for tools." James continued to scroll through the details, muttering as he read, trying to pick through the report for the choicest of info. In the back of the car sat Vikki who, whilst specialising in missing people, was still gelling with the team and wanted to help. We all mucked in when the bell tolled and I was happy for her to expand her wings with us. Anything that betters us as a team got my full support. Except for team away days to do bowling or some other pointless activity.

"How long till we get there boss?" Vikki wanted to know.

"ETA 4 minutes at current speed and conditions," I informed, looking back at her in the rearview mirror for the briefest of seconds. She was smiling at me, seeming to delight in my efficient way of talking for some reason. There was a glint in her eye that seemed playful, but

I had already returned my gaze to the road ahead. Deftly, I might add, I continued without incident to our location and brought the vehicle to a stop without the screech of tires. I knew it was late so I did not want to wake the entire street, so I turned off the sirens when we entered the residential area a few streets back. A man stood outside his home, nonetheless in an ill-fitting pink dressing gown, more than likely belonging to someone else in the house. I surmised this due to the fit, not the preference. 'If you're going to wear something, at least get one that covers your bits,' I concluded. The pink fluffy gown bulged against his weight, but at this point, he was obviously committed to finding out what was happening in his street. Hubbub needed answers. Sergeant Morris was outside the venue already and I nodded a hello to her.

"Jack," she said, affirming my greeting.

"Evening Regan," I replied, knowing her from previous investigations. She turned the other way, as we entered the venue, away to reassure The Pink Panther from across the street and we met a young police constable who was already taking notes from the Victim / Informant / Witness. Vikki moved directly to reassurance mode leaving James to expand on the questions already asked. I was proud of them both already, having taught them to play to their strengths and the pair did it well, their characters a match for each other. Both show the best sides of our team. 'Kind and caring' met 'diligence and investigative' in these two.

As they continued, my eye was drawn to the broken window. It was in the rear of the property which led to an expansive garden shrouded in darkness. I could easily assume that it was well kept as this area would probably oust anyone with a dandelion out of place. Getting nearer, I saw something near the break and moved to examine it further. The window was a traditional wooden frame, painted white more than once. I would always suggest a stronger level of protection but each to their own. Double glazing for heat conservation and tougher on crime prevention all day long.

The frame and glass had not been dusted for forensics yet, but a clump of material caught my eye. Kneeling, I saw that it was a matted clump of long white fur.

## Chapter Six

### The calculating hunter

### The Wolf

Earlier in the evening, as the moon cast its luminous glow over the quiet residential street, a figure padded its way from the shadows, silent and majestic. The light caught and bounced off the white fur and it shimmered under the neon street lamp light, blending with the pale hues of the night. Its piercing silver eyes scanned the surroundings with an air of calculated stealth, alert to every sound and movement. The orbs flowed as neither had pupils, just a fluid mass that danced in the sockets.

With each step, the beast moved with an aqueous grace, aware that its invisibility was its greatest weapon, its paws barely making a sound against the pavement. Muscles rippled beneath the snowy coat, a testament to both its strength and agility. It knew its limits perfectly.

With every sound, its ears flicked back and forth, catching the faintest rustle of leaves or distant hum of electrical activity. The slightest cough from darkened rooms within homes reached it and was noted, then dismissed as to not be its main target.

It was looking for the lone person on their way home. An easy target to such a vicious and calculating hunter. As it traversed the street, the wolf seemed almost ethereal, a ghostly presence drifting through the sleeping neighbourhood. Occasionally, it paused, nose twitching as it sampled the scents lingering in the air, determining its path with uncanny precision.

Despite its imposing size, there was a certain elegance

to the way the wolf moved, a silent predator navigating its territory with ease. As it rounded a corner to yet another residential street, a car was coming from the opposite direction. The beast darted down a wooded alley, frustrated that it had yet to find anything to eat. Hunger was now driving it forward and the barking of a dog drew the beast's attention. Looking towards a brick wall of some height, the wolf heard a small dog yapping from the other side. It angrily barked at the presence of the unknown beast near its boundaries. Then the larger beast vaulted the wall with little effort.

Without a sound, the white-furred creature lunged forward, gripping most of the smaller animal's head in its mouth, immediately silencing any further outbursts. With the barking silent, the limp body of the small dog was wrenched upward violently, to be gulped down with the merest crunch of its small bones to signal its demise. Silence resumed and it took moments to finish its newfound meal, crunching effortlessly through bone and muscle mass. Nothing was wasted, and the white wolf took delicate seconds to lap up the blood that had splashed its thick snowy coat, and the floor. It always made sure to leave no trace of its presence, and more so, no trace of its kill.

The wolf pressed itself against an old pane of glass, wanting to be inside, to find whoever owned its starter course. It hoped for a singular elderly person as they would not put up a fight, making for an easy main course. With unworldly strength, it shattered the glass and the wolf wrenched backwards away from the offending noise. The sound caused more of a cacophony than the beast wanted and it tore itself free of the frame, vaulted the wall, and disappeared back into the night.

With a silent determination, the white wolf continued on its nocturnal journey. Disappearing into the darkness as effortlessly as it had arrived, leaving only the echo of its presence lingering in the stillness of the night.

And a loss to be felt in the morning for the unknowing pet owners.

# Chapter Seven

## The Muffy mystery

### Jack

The area search had brought back a solid no trace and apart from the broken window, no further evidence was making itself apparent. The response unit was then called to another call, that of a drunk driver mistaking a wall for a parking space. (He was all ok, I'm not being glib. Never would, but don't drink and drive, twat). One of the homeowners was looking for her dog around the house as she had definitely heard Muffy drive away the evil intruders. Surmising that the fur was indeed from 'Muffy' the dog, I concluded that it was probably nursing an injury in some dark recess. (I'm more of a cat person myself. I have one. He's called Cat. Because he is one. Plus it seemed to fit. He looked like a cat). Vikki gave dog-based words or advice which went along the lines of, 'he's probably popped out for a poo, now that the windows are broken,' which received a look of horror back from the older man of the house. 'Clearly the gardener,' I thought.

We left them patching the window with cardboard from a discarded Amazon delivery box, its contents long removed. I winced as the tape was placed in a haphazard way and not the correct, and probably more secure, perpendicular. The tape is straight and should be laid as so, but when they didn't iron out the air bubbles. I was near to arresting them for crimes against adhesives. It was a travesty of taping, so I looked away, turning my attention to an old Parker pen I always kept in my pocket to click when needed. It had run out of ink a while ago, but the metallic click-clack helped me in times of chaos.

It was loud enough to feel, but not enough to be heard which stopped all the 'what's that?' lines of enquiry. Occasionally when I was around someone with keener ears, they'd get this befuddled look on their face like they'd left the gas cooker on at home. Vikki, James, and I felt the night shift creep closer to the morning where our upturned lives waited. Such was the call of all night shifts.

"I've always wondered if, at the end of nights, we have breakfast for dinner or the other way round." James wondered out loud as we got back into the car. Vikki giggled tiredly and I pondered the thought.

"If we go to McDonald's and have something from the breakfast menu then it's dinner for us, so it's effectively their dinner menu." I was too tired to work it out efficiently, I just knew that now, he was clearly hungry. So, I googled it.

"5 am their morning menu starts. So, we'll be having their breakfast for our dinner at normal people's breakfast time. Hope that clears that up for you James." Vikki laughed at my logic.

"Sergeant, please call me Jim." I smiled but inwardly I was not going to let two abbreviations bring about the apocalypse, now was I?

"Are we going for team breakfast/dinner then?" I asked the pair.

"I'm dead boss," said James or Jim a little too loudly for all their caffeine-deprived ears.

"We'll see who wants any back at the office," I continued, not wanting to leave anyone out. Except maybe Gareth. Watching him eat was stomach-churning and a great dietary aid for weight loss in others. It was like the green stuffed puppet that lived in the rubbish bin and ate all the cookies or whatever it was. Puppets were not my speciality. When we returned, it was near to finish time and the early turn was already going through handovers and updates from the night shift before. Luckily for them, they were taking over from team four. There was little of note apart from the drunk driver to process and an overly rambunctious hen party that got way out of control. It was Barbie-themed for some reason I could not fathom. Most of the team looked to me like they would collapse where they stood, so I dismissed them with thanks. I made clear to all how much I appreciated their work and they all nodded sleepily back. I even got a weary salute which looked like the dying efforts to swat a fly, but it still counted.

"Are we still getting that non-descript food then boss?" said Vikki from my side once people began filing out. She looked as sprightly as she would starting an early shift and I wondered if I should get her drug tested.

"Fry up? We can hit one of the local Cafés in town? It must be a cafe though, not a caff-a." She said, overly highlighting the French vernacular. She smiled and offered me an elbow, which I shook like a handshake, unsure of what she or I was supposed to be doing at this point. Again, her infectious giggle burst forth.

At the cafe, we both ordered from the set menu, not having the energy to think about our food choices. I went for the healthier option, but it was still a treat nonetheless as all items would be fried to their eventual death. Vikki had taken out her restrained hair and it was now flowing like a labyrinth. Her blonde hair was a mass of wild tangles which danced around each other. It gave her a savage, yet free appearance, and highlighted her slim features. There was a subtle underlying red to it too, which I could see every time she ruffled the wild mass. I looked away awkwardly as she met my eye. God, I hope she didn't think I was checking her out. I'm her boss for God's sake. The paperwork alone... She smiled and looked off in the same direction as I was as our food arrived. We both sat in silence, cradling our coffees as though they were the holiest of liquids. They were, mind you. I began my meal by segregating the different foods, making sure that bean juice was not encroaching on bread, a pet hate of mine. I can be quite forgiving I think, but this was a no. Just, no. Having created a clear eating spot, I looked towards my colleague. Vikki on the other hand had found food at the end of a desert trek and shovelled it in with the abandonment of the starving. It was then that we both realised that we'd left Gareth asleep at his desk.

* * *

Streets away, the sun had risen early that morning as the white wolf returned home. It had eaten its fill of urban denizens and knew that it had once again successfully evaded the prying eyes of human civilization. It had taken its time on a particularly plump cat, although there was no thrill to that chase. It wanted more.

It wanted to hunt the humans.

They were the right prey. They were worthy food.

And so, so tasty.

# Chapter Eight

## The same as all of them.

## The Watcher

Life used to be so pointless, so utterly crushing until that fateful night years ago. All existence before was a dream or a nightmare, owned and lived by another person.

In the dimly lit flat, time seemed to stand still. The occupant's life had been ground gradually down and dwindled into a monotonous routine of wake, work, and sleep if the latter was granted. Each day blurred into the next, leaving him feeling hollow and disconnected from the world around him, an unwilling participant in his limbo. The man sat slumped down on his worn-out couch, the flickering light of the television casting eerie shadows across the room. The silence was suffocating, broken only by the occasional sound of passing cars outside. He ran a hand through his unkempt hair, feeling the weight of loneliness bearing down on him like an invisible anvil, with a scratched-in label that read anxiety.

Even though he wasn't alone.

Once, he had dreams and ambitions that fuelled his days with purpose and excitement, even though he faced failure after failure, as life dealt him a series of blows that left him feeling defeated and directionless. His job at the local pub barely paid the bills, and his social life was now non-existent.

Even though he wasn't alone. He hadn't been for years. He always had someone along for the ride.

As he stared blankly at the TV screen, a sense of despair washed over him like a tidal wave. He wondered how he had ended up here, in this bleak existence where each day had felt like a struggle just to keep his head above water, a turmoil of trauma pulling him ever downwards. Yet despite the darkness that threatened to consume him, there was a flicker, deep within his heart. On one particularly dreary night, his life took an unexpected turn. It gave him a small voice that spoke, lapping at his soul, urging him to keep pushing forward, to believe that better days were ahead.

To be free of the constraints of this world.

To feel the excitement of the hunt.

# Chapter Nine

## Neverending paperwork

### Jack

The next shift passed without incident. I mean a critical one or, even one I'd note as more than our regular day job. There was always something going on in our police world unfortunately. I'd much rather be doing nothing, and everyone is safe than be busy and everyone not. Scratch that. To rephrase, I wouldn't be 'doing nothing.' As that is indeed actually doing something. I'd always endeavour to find something to do, as I loved to make sure that each day, my wages were fully earned. After all, 'people pay taxes which go towards our wages' as the saying often goes. The only thing of note was that there was a report of a terrible car crash on the A3, but it turned out to be on my old ground so our traffic guys, who were all excited to go help, had to turn back. Cross-country command lines were a nightmare of logistics, so their high-viz jackets, little red triangles, and sayings like "you can't park there!" would have to wait.

Days like this were good for catching up on the normal mountainous levels of paperwork. The team were busy going through the evidence from the reported break-in from last night. One of the day shift team had followed up with the homeowner who had not reported anything further that night, although had mentioned that her dog, Muffy, small and fluffy, had not returned home. A Safer Neighbourhood Police Officer and Police Community Support Officer had attended the address and reported that she was more concerned about that than the broken window.

I had some sergeant-based enquiries, and the team were busy filing and making sure i's were centrally dotted, and t's were crossed straight and efficiently.

One of my team was under occupational health having been injured in a fight on duty. She had attended a call at a local venue and the drunk male she was escorting away, thought he was on to a... checks notes... winner. He lent in, and in his words, 'Give us a snog lass! You look fit in that uniform!' which was all captured in glorious evidential 4k body-worn video. He'd even offered his tongue out, lolling it at her which he must've thought was extremely sexy. When she politely declined, he brought both of them crashing to the ground, the crunch audible on the tape. As were my teammate's screams of pain as she had come off worse, landing hip-first on a curb. As it was an injury on duty, I made sure she had the correct recuperation time and helped her with something office-based so she could continue to assist. I've known many officers who, when injured, always wanted to come back too soon so that they don't let the team or the public down. But they forget that they need time to heal so that they can do as such. She was a hard worker and wanted very badly to get back out there, but I was thinking of her first, much to her annoyance. So, among a raft of helpful admin, I also put her in charge of our book club too, as a distraction.

It was designed to build both camaraderie and to take some of the pressure off, as I did not want a burned-out team. I had thought that I had made it clear though, that they should read something light and not police based, yet the meetings always brought some colourful choices...

She opened the meeting of the 'CID Book Club' by saying that we should not discuss CID Book Club. The team laughed, but the reference was completely lost on me. Were we to call it the C.I.D.B.C instead? That sounded like more of a mouthful, but we police did love an acronym. She brought the tale of 'Powerless' by Lauren Roberts. She was yet to start, but 'Booktok' had told her to read it. I thought she had missed the point as it was supposed to be the officer's own choice, but I let it slide. I also didn't know who PC Booktok was as well. Gareth was reading 'Off Season' by Jack Ketchum, a lovely tale of cannibals off the coast of Maine from the 1980's. He explained how grim it was and was delighted to tell the assembled what bit was chopped off and when. I stopped him when he brought the writer's mention of recipes to the group. Vikki was hoovering her way through a book by Sarah J Maas called 'A Court of Thorns and Roses' because, and I am quoting here, she wanted to see if Tamlin and Feyre 'fuck.' She pointed out that the MMC (which apparently stands for Male Main Character) had some clear red flags, but she did not care because he was lush. I don't really know how we communicate sometimes. Jim/James rounded it off with John Marrs 'Keep it in the Family' and was currently on chapter thirty-eight, hoping to settle down after the shift for thirty-nine. I brought 'Of Mice and Men' by John Steinbeck to the table as I thought a 'classic of literature' might be interesting. It wasn't long before I realised that I had violated my guidelines of 'light reading,' but it was worth it.

"What are you doing Jack?" Gareth said suddenly standing over my desk. He was eating a BLT sandwich from the Tesco meal deal, sided with two hard-boiled eggs. He sat on my desk and started pouring salt from a sachet onto the white ovals. Most of it tumbled all over my desk so I brushed it and him into a little corner. I gestured for the DC to sit in a chair that was right beside him, but he missed the urgency of the signal.

"I'm proud of what we've built here Jackie boy. You've become a staple in Surrey CID." He said, stuffing his face with an entire egg. I don't know what confused me more, the statement or the need to eat that whole.

Unfortunately, he continued.

"Mmm ffrr om nom mmm fffrrr." He said eloquently. I couldn't be bothered to work out what he'd said in Eggese, so just nodded in acknowledgement. I was stuck staring at him masticating the poor protein as I had to be ready like a sparring boxer, in case I had to dodge any unexpectedly expelled food. Oh, he was waiting for a reply, I suddenly realised, as he had that 'what do you think?' look in his eyes with his egg-filled mouth.

"I hear what you are saying," I lied in confirmation, hoping for a correct answer. He smiled and I dodged left as food went flying. I nudged the chair again and added in a subtle 'SIT THERE!' head nod. Nope. Still on my desk. So I resorted to extreme methods. In my drawer was a miniature hoover used for clearing keyboards and started to try and 'herd-clean' him into the seat, still watching for flying food.

It was then that I heard an audible giggle, muffled behind a hand. Golden curls were jiggling up and down as were Vikki's shoulders as she stifled a laugh at my expense, clearly watching my torture. She looked back through the jungle of curls, spying on the situation through the tangle. I motioned in my best subtle way for her to save me, but she just beamed further, enjoying Gareth's presence in mine. He was off talking about one of his old cases, regaling it like he was talking about a famous war battle, and his arms were crossed, lost in the detail. I however had locked eyes with the mischievous Victoria, who I would most definitely be having words with! I needed saving and she left me languishing. I smiled back at her and she blushed for reasons unknown to me.

Gareth continued, even though my attention was now very much distracted.

## Chapter Ten

### 'I'm Gay'

### Jim (Or James)

Jim looked over at Gareth and smiled. The older cop had very clearly taken the skipper under his wing, even though the DS had a wingspan to rival the greatest of flights. Jim thought the situation amusing but had great respect for the oafish constable due to a life-changing event a few years before. It had been such an unexpected sentence from the veteran officer, that Jim vowed to always have Gareth's back going forward.

\*\*\*

Jim Hills started where most officers do, on a response team, to learn the craft of policing and find where his talents best suited his career. It was always good to find a niche where internal skills could best be employed to help the public and for some officers, that came down to how much you loved details. A stickler for the minutiae of a single hair might not be able to cope in the ultra-fast-paced world of response but be better suited in the Criminal Investigation Department, or CID, where that was a clear bonus, but start somewhere all did.

One morning as Jim walked into the emergency response team's briefing room, his heart was pounding louder than a siren echoed through the streets. Today was the day he had decided to come out to his colleagues as gay. He had rehearsed the words countless times in his mind, but the fear of rejection still gnawed at him. Would his fellow officers, and his team see him any differently? Would they treat him with the same respect as before? These questions swirled in his mind as he made his way to his seat, his heart pumping in his throat. He wanted to be as open with them as they were with him, and this was the last barrier to achieving it. He considered them family now, so wanted to treat them as he did his own.

Taking a deep breath, Jim finally gathered the courage to share his soul with his colleagues before the morning briefing officially began. Tea and coffee mugs with varying degrees of cleanliness littered the desks on the early shift, some left there from nights, and others were filled with coffee-based goodness. Jim always seemed to remember which officer had which brand for some reason, a detail not relevant to the memory. His voice trembled slightly as he spoke, his palms clammy with nerves. "I have something important to share with all of you," he began, his eyes darting around the room. Officers turned and gave their colleagues their attention, some openly whilst others weren't awake enough for any sort of drama, but it was all there, as this did indeed sound important.

"I'm gay." The words hung in the air, and for a moment, there was silence. Then, to his immense relief, the tension broke as his colleagues erupted into applause. Smiles spread across their faces as they congratulated him on having the strength to pour out his heart in those two single words. Some even offered hugs of support, and it was as if a weight had been lifted off his shoulders. Tears of relief welled up in his eyes and at that moment, he realised that his fears had been unfounded.

Jim remembered seeing the Inspector's face as the outburst of morale filled the room as he entered. Silence fell almost immediately as he walked to the projector as a mark of respect. He was a gruff man of few words and built like the years in the force had crafted his very body. He'd worked in all the roughest boroughs in his career and was described by everyone as having a reputation of being extremely 'ard.' He was the Inspector you didn't want to be at the receiving end of a bollocking, but also the best one when you were in a pickle.

"What's going on, team?" He asked stoically, his voice sounding like granite scraping a bass drum. It was the lead car driver to chime in first before Jim, who was getting himself back into a professional order.

"Jim's just told us he's gay guv, and we were just congratulating him. I mean, I obviously knew." It was a matter-of-fact statement followed by the briefest of beams of pride for his colleague. The Inspector moved to Jim without a sound, his expression the same look of resting vengeful bitch face he always had etched on.

When he got to Jim's side, he embraced him.

"Well done Jim. We're all here for you. Oh, and…" a second passed. "Me too." The room exploded into screams and laughter saved only for family.

As the day went on, Jim was overwhelmed by the outpouring of acceptance from his fellow officers. They treated him with the same camaraderie and respect as they always had, showing him that his sexual orientation didn't change their opinion of him in the slightest. Their unwavering support made him feel truly valued as a member of the team, of their own family. He couldn't help but reflect on how fortunate he was to work in such an inclusive environment, shocked at his precognition of what would happen. He knew that not everyone was as lucky, and he felt a sense of gratitude towards his colleagues for their understanding and acceptance. Coming out had been one of the most nerve-racking experiences of his life, as his own dad had taken a long time to fully accept it, but when he did, it had been incredibly empowering.

As he prepared to leave the shift as a new, and free officer, Jim remembered that he couldn't wipe the smile off his face. He felt lighter, happier, and more confident than he had in years.

He was out-out now.

And as he bid farewell to his colleagues, he knew that he was no longer just a police officer—he was a proud gay police officer, supported by an incredible team. Especially that area car driver, who was transferring to CID next week.

Gareth had his back that day.

It was a day he wished he could travel back to.

# Chapter Eleven

## Body language matters

### Vikki

Detective Constable Vikki Doherty sat on the arm of the sofa to try and reassure the crying parent sitting across from her. She knew that posture was everything as open body language was one of the best weapons an officer could deploy.

She knew her sitting placement could add to the seriousness of the situation unfolding and leaned down from her perch to add intensity and care to her words. The wrong body language could turn any situation on a sixpence in policing, so it is always foremost in the young officers' thoughts. Vikki knew that standing sent the wrong message and sitting on the sofa was too informal and lacked urgency, so she was opting for a midground approach. Being completely standing said quite clearly that this case wasn't important as she wasn't staying, ergo didn't even care. This was completely not the case though and Vikki wanted to express it outwardly. Sitting down on a sofa was a minefield of visual issues and could be seen as too relaxed and uncaring, especially if the sofa was a comfy one. It was human nature to relax, especially when faced with stress and anxiety, so the 'perch position' always mixed the two to great effect. It showed that this was the ONLY case of import, which was paramount to parents of missing children, so her playbook of caring was dutifully played out.

Sit to show import, but not enough that it was comfy. Tick.

Lean in to show that she was listening to every

syllable, which she of course was. Tick.

Sit in an uncomfortable location to show that she was ready to bolt should the emergency need arise. A tick once more.

"We will try everything possible to find your daughter, Mrs Simpson. Officers are out looking even as we speak. I cannot imagine what you are going through but I need to get any further information to the teams searching. Do you mind if I ask you to confirm everything you said in the 999 call? Mainly concerning what she was wearing when she left?" Vikki said everything calmly but made sure her voice conveyed the care she was feeling. She was cautious not to use the phrase 'What was Mia last seen wearing?' as it conveyed a finality to the matter.

It had connotations.

Vikki had done this routine far too many times, unfortunately, but all were as important as the last. A specialist in missing people, she understood both their reasons for disappearing and how they'd go about it.

All too well.

Luckily in most cases, the missing loved one, or 'misper' for short, would return on their own having blown off whatever emotional steam had boiled to the top. Others were located with the help of the general public, and even more by officers simply searching.

Very few turned up deceased.

But some did. Those were usually the ones committed to self-harming and time was as critical an asset as manpower. If a misper wanted to do it, we'd normally find them at the point they've done it. Every one of them hurt Vikki. She wanted them all to be saved, to, at that most desperate of points, find that lifeline. It could be a friend, or family member that caught the signs, or even a stranger. It would be just enough. That small spark that life wants them around.

The hardest ones though, were when there were no signs whatsoever. People who hid their darkness deep down for when they were sure that they were alone, behind a facade of smiles and laughter. These struggling people would both subconsciously and unconsciously meticulously conceal the storm raging within them. Every day in their lives would become a performance, a delicate dance of feigned happiness to shield loved ones from the shadows lurking in their hearts. Behind every closed door was a battle against a relentless tide of despair, buried anguish beneath layers of pretence. Laughter would echo hollowly, a fragile mask disguising turmoil. Fearful of burdening those they cherish, pain would be locked away, imprisoned within a fortress of their own silence.

Yet, the weight of hidden sorrow would still grow heavier with each passing day, as the invisible burden they bore alone festered, hidden away from the comforting embrace of oblivious loved ones. In all these cases, these people would resonate through the teams on and off duty as there was more often than not an absolutely zero chance of helping. It left officers with the nagging annoyance that they wished the person in need had reached out before the devastating act, without blaming the poor victim but more that help was out there and left unasked for.

Vikki felt herself remembering the lost ones and pinched herself back to reality. A misper needed her.

"Anything you can add to her last…" She rephrased quickly, realising the tangent, which fortunately was missed by the parents of the lost. She was very clearly thinking more about her own words than they were at this time, which was understandable, Vikki surmised.

"Does she have friends she might go to? Any hangouts, groups, or places, other than here obviously, that she would consider safe? Can I also confirm exactly what she was wearing when she left?" Vikki wanted to know all she could as any detail might be the jigsaw puzzle piece she needed.

"Social media accounts? Do you have a list?" Vikki wanted to know. Mia's mother nodded and started writing them down as best she could, fumbling with her phone to find the details.

The playbook seemed to be working as planned and Mrs Simpson wiped away a snuffled sob, moving to concentrate on answering the questions. She collected her thoughts, dwelling on the inquiries, and Vikki watched her mind actively work behind her eyes. She was grasping for any missed detail, anything that could help her helpers. As the mother tried to recall the details, her eyes darted about as if processing data on a screen.

Vikki looked around the room while she thought, taking in any details of note that might assist with the search. It was a standard living room with average trimmings. The sky box was neatly placed within an Ikea television stand, alongside a collection of old remotes that hadn't been thrown out with the even older equipment. Pictures of their family at various life stages were littered about various sideboards, which gave Vikki the impression that the misper, Mia, seventeen, white, female, seen (last) wearing jeans and a t-shirt, was loved.

Mia's father, Kevin Simpson, hadn't moved or said anything the entire time the CID officers had been there. Initially, Vikki had thought that this was odd, peculiar even, so she examined his demeanour for anything evidential.

His hands were bloodless due to the grip he had on his knees. A raging vein pulsed in his temple. A slight shake in his jawline. The brow in the centre of his head was furrowed ever so slightly. Vikki made a controlled eye contact, allowing her features to soften in as supportive a fashion as possible. When their eyes met, he crumpled, and tears streamed down his cheeks, a river flowing with grief.

No words needed to be said and Vikki nodded slightly, acknowledging that he had been using all his strength for his wife, to the point of actual, physical pain. He was trying to be strong, showing the courage that he thought his wife needed, but Vikki's look showed him that he could crumble. It was allowed and encouraged. He too was allowed to pour out his emotions, but was clearly from the generation where he was only told to 'man up.' Kevin collapsed into his hands showing him as the loving parent who was missing his little girl. Vikki took strength from his pain which she funnelled directly into her need to find Mia for them both. Stepping to his side, she reassured him by gently gripping his upper arm, not wanting to press any boundaries, but doing enough that the human contact brought the older man the courage that he needed. He brought his hand up to hers and their eyes met again and as Kevin's gaze met Vikki's, it said a clear 'thank you' without a sound uttered.

Information had started flowing now, but it was joined by countless; "Sorry to waste your time, she's probably fine." Excuses were being made, that didn't need to be made. Mia was missing. Question it when she was safe.

"Mrs Simpson. Louise. Is it ok to call you that? Firstly, keeping your loved ones safe is never a waste of anyone's time, especially ours. Ever. Secondly, we'll do our utmost to ensure that she is returned home. Officers are already searching." Vikki's words were that of a police officer who cared, and in every fibre of her being, she meant it.

And it showed.

Louise stood immediately and hugged Vikki with an emotion that gushed forth. It was almost a relief felt too soon but it's what the older women needed at that moment. She seemed to deflate in Vikki's embrace and she made sure the older woman was supported both literally and figuratively. This was not the time to get the London Ambulance Service out for a collapse at this point.

Mia was in need. And Vikki was the one to give it.

## Chapter Twelve

### The reason behind the runner

### Mia

The room where support and answers were now flowing freely, was telling a very different story than it did the night previous. Desperation had replaced anger, sobs substituting shouts. Mia looked across at her parents who were trying to engage her in the 'University conversation' once again. On and on they would go, and it annoyed Mia exponentially higher with each passively aggressive pamphlet left on the table or question added into every conversation. Every time they tried to force her in their chosen direction, she would travel further to the other. She knew better than any prospectus as the seventeen-year-old girl thought nothing of higher education and wanted, no, planned to become the next online sensation any way she could. She was owed it.

It would happen. It was within her grasp. Be it an Instagram influencer or YouTube star, she would throw all her efforts in that direction. It was working to a point too as her analytics screamed an ever-increasing journey to the top. A rising star on TikTok, her followers were joining faster than she could engage with, although, with the current 'scandal' of music restrictions on the platform, she was finding it hard to trend as she used to.

And should be trending right now, but no. School talks once again. She sighed audibly at the two people holding her back the most, letting her frustration out as a sign of contempt. She wanted to be in her comments section, as even they knew better than her parents and were pushing her more into the corners of social media.

Even though at times it was a sewer, with lecherous men proposing the most hideous of things, she dove into the influencer life. Initially, she had reported every trollish comment, spewed forth from grown men who she imagined were nestled in their mother's basements, but their numbers continued to grow and her time dwindled. She gave up all thoughts of moderation a few months ago as the behind-the-scenes work was taking her away from in front of the camera. She concluded that her audience was being bolstered by these trolls, so allowed them in.

The lesser of two evils.

Her content revolved around her looking into the camera as the LED circular glare highlighted her beauty as she commented on current trends or reacted to other users' content in side by side split screen. Mia was regularly called beautiful, and even spectacular, as her long brown hair flowed, seemingly blowing and swishing even when there was no wind to capture it. It framed her blue eyes perfectly, portraying her as the essence of the modern youth aesthetic. The comments gushed and brought the likes and requests for more. Always more.

Her career choice had not gone down very well with the adults in the room though who tried to tell her that 'it wasn't a real job' and that they 'couldn't afford to carry her.' They'd moaned on about her getting a proper job first and then expanding to something more 'frivolous' when she was financially stable. They even dared to tell her to get a job as an admin in a related industry, but she was above bringing coffee to media execs.

Frivolous? They didn't understand her. Too old.

'Gen Z is now, Gen X is a bag of pants' She thought,

wondering if she could get that trending. She noted that it would be best to just call them Boomers and be safe, even though she didn't understand the terms precisely. She'd heard all the terms in trending videos and hoped she was using them correctly. She'd never been pulled up, so concluded she was. 'Boomers would trend easier than something she'd made up,' she thought, knowing the labels were an easy win online. Frivolous had been the word that had been the trigger, as her dream was not to be considered a flight of fancy. Both her parents wanted her to use the more traditional skills as she excelled in Maths, getting the highest GCSE grade possible. This in turn brought top marks in other linked subjects including all the sciences making her journey to university one of the easiest imaginable.

She had stormed out at that point, shouting her hatred venomously at both her parents. It was said out of spite, in anger, and not meant wholly, but said it was nonetheless. As she left, she heard her mother crying and regretted her choice immediately, but going back on it now would let them take a win and would push her away from her burgeoning career.

Sadness began to fill her heart and she felt the first tear fall.

It was a feeling she did not hold for long.

## Chapter Thirteen

### A second set of eyes

### The Watcher

'The night hides its secrets well,' thought the beast as it padded silently around the darkened areas of the park.

It was one of two figures hidden there as the world slept around them, with one being considerably more dangerous than the other. Under the cloak of the moonlit night, the white-haired creature moved with an inky, calculated grace through the shadowed depths of the expansive park. Its oyster-coloured fur seemed to blend seamlessly with the darkness, rendering it nearly invisible amidst the long-shadowed areas. Even being achromatic, the creature's enhanced stealth abilities rendered it almost a shadow in the undergrowth. Years it had hunted and it knew how to disappear when it needed to.

It never wanted to be seen. Being seen brought the storm.

It brought death, and many of its kin had fallen foul of the light.

Due to the hour, the air felt heavy and hung with an ominous stillness as the beast waited, its eyes gleaming as the pinpricks of light bounced off the silver fluid-filled orbs. In nature they appeared rather otherworldly as the seemingly metallic fluid sloshed inside the case of the eyeball, dancing with only a hint of blue to show life. The two pearl-like lanterns watched their prey, stalking the target they had chosen.

It hunted with unwavering determination, calculating

both risk and reward with each action. Each silent step left barely a whisper as it approached, a phantom of the urban wilderness. Occasionally a streetlight's brilliance would dance upon the sleek fur, revealing a labyrinth of scars that bore testament to countless encounters in its past expeditions. But then, without a sound, it would disappear once more into the noir void, dancing in and out of the darkness. Its senses, finely tuned and keenly aware, locked onto the subtlest of movements.

The other being with the beast was a humanoid and as such was easier to blend in with the other humans, but it lurked with the creature it felt connected to. He'd learned in the role of watcher to be as invisible as the beast at his side. He was the observer, the keeper, the host and the cleaner. In the dimly lit confines of the tree-lined park, the Watcher skulked in silent communion with his loyal companion, the majestic white wolf. He stood low, hiding at the rear flank of the beast, with one hand on its hind quarters. He felt the power under his fingers as the moon cast its ethereal glow upon the pair as a feverish excitement ignited within them both, reflected in the gleam of predatory eyes. The man's fingers trembled with anticipation, tracing the contours of the flank muscle with a fervour bordering on obsession. With each passing moment, his pulse quickened, fuelled by the exhilarating prospect of the kill. Beside him, the white wolf sensed his host's growing fervour, his primal instincts stirring in tandem. Together, they were a lethal symbiosis, united in their insatiable hunger for blood. In the shadowed depths of the night, their bond forged in darkness years before, they awaited the call of their next unsuspecting victim, their anticipation swelling with each passing heartbeat.

And then they saw their target.

They saw her.

It was a girl. No more than seventeen. She was crying, but talking into her phone, blissfully unaware of the eyes watching. She had no thought of the impending danger, distracted into a blissful ignorance.

'All of the cattle tasted similar,' the wolf thought idly, but the level of toughness of the meat was what brought out the sweetness in the meal. Too much muscle would make it chewy and rubbery, like eating a screaming, blood-soaked tyre.

'She would be perfect though,' concluded the creature who was trying to run tactical attack options in its head, failing dismally as the raw emotion of the kill controlled all incoming actions. It had not eaten many humans before as they often fought back and if the kill was not certain, the aftermath would bring further troubles.

Humans, whilst tasty, brought with them chaos. As the white hair of the entity drew closer, the park seemed to hold its breath, anticipating the imminent dance of predator and prey beneath the moon's watchful gaze. It would be lion and mouse though on this night, as the beast, eager to taste the hot coppery fluid coursing down its throat approached.

And the second set of eyes watched on just as eagerly, his smile manically wide.

The wolf licked its lips as the watcher looked on.

## Chapter Fourteen

### Unsocial media

### Vikki

"I just don't know why they don't listen! They don't even follow my TikTok! Have they watched any of my lives? No! Do they even finish my content? No!" Mia said, rather over-exaggerating her emotions for the camera and the unseen audience behind her social media platform. This was a 'hype' drama she could capitalise on, and she was preaching to a highly converted, media enrapt congregation. She watched as the hearts tumbled in, flowing up on her screen like praise-filled rain and she tried to muffle her smile. Mia made sure the angle of the camera was high so she could enhance the fabricated vulnerability of her situation, and she took moments, brief teasing seconds, to look longingly into the lens, as the tears of a crocodile brought more engagement.

Rosebury Park was picturesque in the day, with glorious willow trees and long walks you could lose yourself in, but at night under the flickering lamplight, it held an eerie quiet that was wondrous for filming. Hidden from the street by an immaculately kept hedgerow, the orange hue highlighted Mia's face as she walked past the children's play area. She toyed with sitting there, as the swings would add to the look of vulnerability. As she approached, she noticed that there was a hooded teenager already moping backwards and forward on the play equipment. He was smoking a joint, which carried the waft of the all too familiar smell of cannabis and she didn't much want real-world company anyway. They would see behind the online facade and she couldn't risk being exposed as some sort of digital fraud. That was a cybernated trauma she could well do without.

After wandering through the darkened pathways, she chose to sit not far from the main high street. During the day it was filled with shoppers who would park on weekdays to fill their bags with treasures from the collection of shops. At this hour though it was just the nightlife bustling past, unaware of the girl sitting near them.

Comments flowed up on her screen as they consoled, cajoled and craved. It was a mixed bag of musing from her followers as they had not seen her upset, but more worryingly, without makeup.

Gary_2002 commented that he 'still would' adding an aubergine emoji to show his apparent readiness, but it was drowned out by a menagerie of followers agreeing with Mia's predicament. Hearts pinged consistently up the screen as the live viewing count rose considerably. Gary_2002 added in a fist emoji and then droplets of water which were next to the digital tacho, but even this art form of graphic filth was swallowed up by the comment stream. Seeing the number ticking up brought a smile to her face but she quickly squashed it so that she could stay in the character of a wounded teen, held back from her beloved audience.

A slight movement to the right distracted her, and she looked past the phone and off into the darkness. There was nothing. Just blackness. Then the briefest glimpse of something silver or, possibly white. 'No, it's nothing' she thought, trying not to look away from the lens. A few of the commenters picked up on her distraction, even though it was the briefest of flickers. They knew that her attention was not one hundred per cent on them and they didn't like it. Gary_2002 returned and shouted in full caps locked anger;

"WHAT R U LOOKING AT?!" No fruits or vegetables were employed this time, just a clear indication of anger and annoyance due to the capitalised emphasis. Mia ignored him and continued her feigned pain, her attention back once more to her invisible audience.

"They should be supporting me! I'm going to be Insta big and I want you all with me. We'll party and…" The words faltered as a movement again caught her attention. It was closer this time and just enough to make her worry that she was not as alone in the park as she thought.

"Tell me where u r. I'll cum save u." Gary_2002 offered un-gallantly. Mia was unsure whether Gary would be a help or hindrance but she worried nonetheless. Others were joining in the distraction dilemma now, trying to find out why Mia was not talking anymore, and more so what she was trying to see off-camera. Some started saying that this was an act, or a stunt, to gain further attention, adding to the chattering confusion.

"Mia, Bae, you're still live!" Said one supporter in the hope that she would return to the feed, but Mia was squinting into the night now. The phone dipped slightly and the viewing camera angle changed to slightly under her chin, showing mostly stars and the lamplight above. It obscured the viewpoint as it flashed and flickered. The audience could see mostly night sky now, as the camera dipped further away from the influencer they had tuned in for. The comments were all concerning now. Even Gary_2002 had lost interest and disappeared from the rapidly appearing conscious stream.

Mia looked forward as a rush of fur ripped into the camera view.

***

The beast took the girl down with ease, hardly even a challenge and barely a sound on initial impact.

She'd fallen hard on the concrete pavement near the seat where she was broadcasting, and the force had knocked the camera away. It scuttled three feet from her, clattering on the floor, ending up near a hedge, metres away. The live feed abruptly blinked out of existence leaving those with countless questions left unanswered.

Had it still been filming; the audience would have been auditory witnesses. They would have heard the crack of Mia's skull on the pavement, the crunch of bone and the tearing of flesh as the creature killed, and then ate its prey.

After the initial impact, her whimpers dwindled as Mia drew her last, gurgling, breath..

## Chapter Fifteen

### The watcher in the woods

As the beast ate, the watcher sloshed water on the pathway, clearing the blood from obvious sight. The wolf took his time, savouring each torn morsel from the body in front of him. The creature, who had been affectionately called 'White' lapped at the blood, trying not to leave any around as he savoured the coppery taste on his tongue. The fluid was now a new lifeblood in the wolf's body, and he enjoyed the warmth he felt deep within.

The scarlet splatter in the long grass was tougher to clean, and both the watcher and the wolf hoped for rain. The cleansing downfall of water would make their job a lot easier and as the clouds gathered their two smiles appeared. One carried a hint of pleasure at the fact that it would wash away their human sin, but the other? It was wide and unfaltering. Manic even.

Hunting the humans was risky.

And both enjoyed that. Both loved the fact that they were the apex predator in this town. No one else came close.

This was how it should be.

Wolf and Watcher, together, culling the herd, for food and pleasure. It wasn't always like this though, and they had to learn to live with each other since the change.

The watcher remembered the sequence of events that led the two killers together, and his smile broadened. A laugh burst forth and White turned and snarled at the sound, causing a hand to clamp shut the outburst of insanity. The wolf returned to feeding, lowering itself to hide its presence further into the shadows. Stifled into silence, the only sound heard was the crunching of bone and slurping of tissue as the wolf ate.

The watcher would sometimes pleasure itself on the prey if caught before devoured. This time that would be an impossibility. There was no earthly way in the state she was in now, that that could happen. The white wolf was ravenously hungry and wanted to eat every delicious morsel. It wasn't sharing. Pleasure aside, the voracious hunger would leave nothing whatsoever albeit aiding the clean. 'Swings and roundabouts' thought the watcher, who wanted everything pristine, because tearing a human being apart was a very messy business. There would be blood everywhere as it had a tendency to spray when bitten in haste. The true crime shows, CSI's and whodunnits had helped greatly in their desire to evade capture. No one had come close to realising what was happening in the quiet, sleepy town of Epsom and its surrounding boroughs. Killing cross borders helped with keeping their activities in the shadows, as the greatest of serial killers had the foresight to not shit on their own doorstep too much.

'White would be mostly Red at this point' observed the Watcher who remembered that cleaning such a massive beast was always tricky. But they made it work. They'd always been in the shadows ever since they met that fateful night. The Change. They both remembered it fondly as it would forever alter their existence in this world, as one was born, and the other renewed with a glorious purpose.

Prior to the change, the watcher was an outcast, shunned by society as weak, a loner. People would avoid any interactions with him at seemingly all costs and loneliness built like an empty palace.

The solitude felt like a grayscale landscape, devoid of colour, filled with shadows. It was a desolate and agonising experience, as every day was a world drained of its vibrancy, where hues faded into a lifeless monotony. In this absence of colour, every interaction, every moment felt hollow and devoid of warmth. It hurt him inside to be alive. It caused him pain to breathe, each life-giving lungful an absolute effort. A battle of pointless existence. There was no one. Emptiness. Nothing. A desolation of seclusion from which he just wanted to be heard. By someone, by anyone. He tried to have an online presence, but even the comfort of strangers alluded him. This barren wasteland, where the once vivid palette of life in its untarnished youth, had been replaced by a dreary void.

And at this low point, was where he had met the Grey one.

It was years ago now.

1993 to be exact.

They both remembered and smiled at the chance encounter, and diligently, they went back to their tasks of disposing of the once full-of-life, Mia.

## Chapter Sixteen

### Back in 1993

The long walk home from work was always the toughest on Fridays. Tending bar in the dilapidated pub was not ideal, but it served a purpose for Nathan to get out of the house. His parents would constantly berate him to 'be a better person' or 'go out and get married' as if either would change the remoteness of his life. His work was the best chance to get any action though, preying on drunk patrons left over by the other customers, but even they avoided the bar staff. Avoided him, mainly. 'Couldn't even give it away,' he'd think nightly. Getting lucky was simply not happening.

Also, whilst the staff acknowledged that there was another member of the team talking to them, he was still made to feel like an outcast to the other teammates. Never invited to any of the out-of-office gatherings, and never included in the Secret Santa gift exchanges either for that matter. He was a shadow in the hospitality world and often scoffed at the irony. It was getting to the point of maliciousness. He didn't know why they, or the world for that matter, hated him so much. He'd think back on his life and try to bring to the forefront the memory of some heinous act where he'd murdered a child, or something just as hideous causing him to earn this treatment from the entire populace.

But there was nothing. He was nothing. Nobody.

The loneliness was crushing. Only being spoken to when speaking directly in someone's eyeline became a habit as when he was 'off camera,' people would actively avoid responding, much like they would do to someone with leprosy.

But unbeknownst to all, an application, sent in secret, for the new 'All Bar One' which was due to open next year had been submitted. Yes, it was opening in December but waiting was now a skillset, having nothing else to live for anyway. Nathan hoped to upgrade from the front counter to assistant manager, to make it impossible for people to not directly converse. If he was in charge, they'd simply have to.

Fuck them all.

For all the 18 years of his life, Nathan had languished in this crushing loneliness, sitting stewing in a cauldron of despair that with each day added more emotional ingredients. Anger had tainted the dish as the silence in the world weighed heavily on his overburdened shoulders, each passing second echoing the isolation louder than before. Fists would clench unconsciously when sitting in the staff room of the pub, nails digging into palms as frustration bubbled within like a tempest ready to erupt. With each breath, the weight of his meagre life expectations crushed down on him, suffocating him in a world that seemed indifferent to the struggles of solitariness.

Longing for connection and craving what he wanted so, very badly. He believed this contact was due even, a deserved standard human feeling, or need. Just for someone to understand the storm raging inside, to be there to listen, to hear and to hold, was all he'd ever wanted. But all that remained was the emptiness of the surroundings. Anger became his only companion, a bitter reminder of bonds craved but he could never seem to forge. Life had been unnecessarily hard and something had to be coming over the horizon that would change everything. For the better. Something had to happen. Something... Anything...

Something owed for the years of being bullied at school.

Something owed for the years of being left in the darkness.

The walk homeward to Cheam was normally brisk as the relative safety of the ground floor flat offered brief respite. He could go to his room and just hide away from it all. Nathan had been mugged on this same route, the muggers had stolen trinkets, and nothing much of value as Nathan had neither wealth nor items of worth. This early evening in 1993 brought the second mugging. Two males and one female on the way home after a lunchtime beer session offered a drunken opportunity of slurred sex, and Nathan considered the opportunity. It turned out that the stench of alcohol was too much, even in his desperate state. One of the men had vomited down his shirt too which removed all romance from the situation. In better circumstances, he would've taken any of them, just for the feeling of being with someone, but this was too much, even for him.

He was pushed up against a wall, the lead drunk trying to pull in close for a kiss, but Nathan instinctively pushed the keys into the reddened face, catching on a flared nostril.

"Frigid! Come on, we can take turns on this one." They slurred as they left motioning to the female among them who was laughing raucously.

Their final act of drunken annoyance was to launch

the offending keys into the darkness. It was the most hurtful part of the incident, as it had added a full thirty minutes to his walking time, having to hunt for his keys and it brought the streets of Cheam into view at just before seven.

Currently the most annoying. That was about to change.

Chatsworth Road was normally quiet for foot traffic, but loud for cars. It was a quick cut-through en route to Epsom and onwards to New Malden then on to Kingston. But at this late hour, lights were filling the streets. Looking down the darkened path to Cheam High School, lights in the car park could be clearly seen by parents who waited for their offspring for something he knew not of.

A scream ripped through the night as the shadowed outlines of bodies that he could see were now furtive, running around in a panic. Something was very wrong.

More movement.

Furtive and fleeing.

The passage was dark and the lights of the cars obscured Nathan's vision, and it was also cloaking the dark fur of the fleeing creature running down the access path.

Toward him. By the time it reached him, it was too late.

Leaping, the grey-furred thing used the body in its fleeing path as a springboard, fleeing the lights and clamour of the collected cars. Claws raked down Nathan's chest, rending his skin painfully under his coat. Whilst not deep, the feeling of the hot stickiness of the blood starting to dampen the shirt filled his senses.

The smell hit hard. Like wet copper.

He yelped in pain but it was fleeting as another injury distracted him. The beast's teeth caught on an earlobe, wrenching most of it away from the head, in its flight into the night. Then the grey-furred creature was gone. Up and away into the darkness, as quick as it had been, it was now a memory. The assailant left, leaving Nathan a bloodied mess sitting by the roadside, bleeding from all his open wounds.

Luckily, none of them seemed life-threatening and he tended to them as best possible. Mainly focussed on stemming the bleeding and within minutes, an ambulance appeared. Nathan beamed, thankful that some unknown worried witness must have called from their home, eager to help the wounded man in the darkness. 'Someone had actually, cared,' he thought, tears of happiness mingling with the ones that streaked the pain. Rising as the large yellow and green vehicle entered the passage, a hand was raised gingerly to attract their attention.

But the ambulance continued down the path, till it was awash with the headlights in the car park.

Even they could not see.

Even they avoided him.

The feeling of loneliness returned with a sledgehammer.

"I'm alone," came the words as desperation and pain flooded through his injured body.

He was truly alone.

For now.

Grey went back into hiding that night. His risk, whilst nourishing brought a threat it had not faced before.

Humans.

They would hurt Grey. They would hunt Grey.

So it hid in the shadows for years, only venturing out when hunger called again, and even then it would be a household pet, or a rat. It longed for the taste of human flesh once more. And when the streets fell silent between 2020 and 2021, Grey's courage returned.

The streets were its playground once more.

And again it hunted.

Again it hungered...

# Chapter Seventeen

## The search begins...

### Vikki

Vikki sat in the car as Jim drove. They were targeting places that they thought would be where a young person would frequent. They were mainly open and public areas because if Mia was in a house? That would make the search virtually impossible from a passenger car seat unless actionable intelligence had been gained. If she was being hidden by others, finding her would be tantamount to a haystack filled with needles and you're trying to find the blunt one. Marked units were checking relatives and friends, leaving the CID unmarked car to area search. Currently, there was no trace on all fronts.

Area searching relied on three things.

⅄ Intelligence and guesswork based on the missing person

⅄ A copper's nose

⅄ A shitload of luck

Vikki's job phone rang, and she hoped option three would be paying off soon.

"I called George's, Chelsea and Westminster, and the other one. St Helier. Over Sutton way. I had my hernia fixed there." Said DC Gareth Derby informing her of the local hospitals he had rang. Plus, obviously, the extra info was completely irrelevant, and she heaved a little, as her mind generated an image of the older constable in those tiny hospital pants that left little to the imagination. It was standard procedure to check all local A&Es in case of mishap, and while Gareth was in the office anyway,

Vikki was going to use him. She also made sure that he'd check if anyone had shown up without identification as that was also sometimes a lucky, or unlucky depending on the situation, catch. Vikki had had a misper once storm out, much the same as Mia, with the full intent to harm himself but had, luckily for everyone, botched the job. He'd then groggily been picked up by an eagle-eyed ambulance team who got him to a place of safety, that being their hospital. No ID on him meant that he was a John Doe, so the description was checked and options two and three had won the day.

'Sniff, sniff!' thought Vikki, recalling the rescue.

"The skipper's on his way out to you guys, Vik, get your hair up before Mr Stickler gets a cork up his arse!" Gareth's voice interrupted her recollection, and she felt herself blush at the thought of seeing the Detective Sergeant.

Ever since their first meeting, she had felt a longing for him, as she had never met anyone quite like Jack. He was so rigid in his ways, but the caring undercurrent in his actions showed him to be a true leader and someone you'd want in your corner. She wanted him alright. In the corner, on the floor, on the side, anywhere. But he was professional, and so was she, so she kept him at arm's length. It was getting hard though. 'Hard,' she giggled at the word in her thoughts. 'So childish Vik,' she scolded, giggling again.

It was then that she realised that Gareth was still on the phone.

"Keep trying please mate. Anything else you get, let me know. Oh, also, send it down to everyone's box please?" Box meant the small computer in each of the cars so that the teams could access Mia's picture immediately, but she still giggled at the word 'box.' Vikki had a childish sense of humour with words, and even at times of stress, found amusement. It was a humour out of necessity though as the anxiety each case brought could crush a person without such an outlet. Some officers played sports on their rest days others though, bottled it all up. She hung up on Gareth as he had nothing more to add and she wanted him searching from his vantage point. She returned her attention to the road, walkways, the alleys, and everywhere she thought a person could linger, paying particular attention to any shadowed areas. Jim broke the silence first.

"You like the skipper don't you Vik?" His words cut through the car like paparazzi through gossip and she looked at him agog.

"We're all coppers Vik, it's fine. Nothing gets past us." Jim didn't make eye contact as he was multitasking both driving, searching and chatting.

"Look, we're both similar ages, and I totally get where you're coming from. He's fit as fuck, if a little weird." Jim took the opportunity to express this thought as a way to open up to Vikki and show that he meant no malice to her. She closed her mouth as the shock of the two sentences reverberated around the car, leaving long moments of incredulous silence hanging in the air.

"So, I know you're gay, but I didn't realise that you had a crush too!" She realised that her last sentence made them sound like school kids crushing on the same bae. Briefly, they looked at each other and burst out laughing simultaneously, whilst still searching like hawks to prey. The moment bonded the pair, and they relaxed in each other's company shortly afterwards, both knowing the secret crush they had on the stoic skipper.

Still no trace. Still they searched. Even though the pair had taken a respite with chatting, it did not detract from the search at hand, and the thought of it jerked the morale from the car.

Both wanted to find Mia. Alive preferably.

Safe, almost definitely.

# Chapter Eighteen

## Empty hands and hearts

### Jack

The search was coming up empty at this point as both intel leads and all the local copper's knowledge available to us were drawing crushing blanks.

'Luck was all that was left,' I thought, hating the element of chance. This was not the science and evidential basis of policing I strove for, but to save a life, I would employ it.

"Luck is an accident," I said out loud, to no one else in the car. I'd managed to borrow an older vehicle which was always the one left till last every shift as it was not 'blues and twosey' enough. This meant that there was no junk in the engine as the popular saying goes. I had no 'need for speed' though, as I was much more interested in stealth and this car was perfect. The Vauxhall Astra. If it wasn't a souped-up boy toy, then it was something Grandad drove, and certainly not a copper on the lookout for a missing child. I corrected my statement to 'young adult,' as getting the wrong title was disrespectful. We needed rapport at this point, which is why Vikki was perfect. She had a way with people and her smile warmed the coldest of hearts, a skill I believed I was lacking in.

If jobs and lives were different, I might have even tried courting her or asking her to the cinema, whatever dating was nowadays in today's society. It all seemed lost on me, as I was useless with women. I don't mind admitting it. Don't get me wrong, I've had intercourse relationships, but more when I didn't realise it was going to happen.

Let me explain.

I think three, four, ten steps ahead of people. And what I mean is that I play out conversations and all their possible answers before they are even uttered. It works wonders in suspect interviews, but when on a date, it gets weird very quickly. I'd play out everything without the thought of spontaneity factoring in, so when a woman finds me attractive, due to my physique and not the awkward silences, I'd wind up in a bathroom having the 'hankiest of panky' before I realised what was occurring.

My relationships wouldn't last thereafter as I quickly would find out that my long work hours and bumbling conversation skills did not eclipse the nookie or toned runner's body. It's fine though. I didn't crave attention when there was work that needed to be done. If I slipped, lives could be lost, so keeping the weight on my shoulders allowed others the dalliances of normal life.

I had Cat and that was enough.

Or so I thought.

I would describe Vikki as my polar opposite. Where I was calm and collected, she was lively and bubbly. Where I would put the pen lid back on the writing tool, she'd jam it in those dazzlingly delightful curls, often walking home with one or two, still jammed in there, such was their wild abandonment.

Yes, she was a mess, but a gorgeous one, internally and externally. Yet she had the same tendencies as my current nemesis, Gareth. Both their desks were in a complete state, but Vikki had brought in her own stapler meaning she was trying to be organised, if just a little. I chose to let her off a bit. It had a unicorn on it for some reason. It just seemed to make everything ok. She made everything ok. (Even though it was not Met issue where mine was very much so). She was such a distraction, which I would stifle down as the job was all important.

'Must not fall,' I chided myself for letting the barrier slip. She was a work colleague and that was that. I drove around for what seemed like an hour, trying to think like myself and not the wonderful Vikki, this way, we'd cover different areas of the ground. She'd searched Epsom Common under the guidance of the NPAS helicopter as one of the nearest green spaces, so I chose other popular park-based locales. She'd been joined by marked units as the Common was extensive, which made the helicopter a necessity. I heard over the radio that they had enough units, so my team went off to another venue. Good thinking Vik, spread the resources.

As I sifted through the evidence board in my head, my thoughts raced with urgency and precision, each task a calculated step towards finding Mia. With my normal methodical determination, I checked off leads, my mind a flurry of potential scenarios and outcomes. Every piece of mental information was scrutinised, in the hope that it would bring us closer to unravelling the mystery of her disappearance. Yet, amidst the chaos of the misper investigation, there was always a nagging sense of responsibility that weighed heavily on my shoulders.

Mia's face, innocent and vulnerable, haunted my thoughts, driving me to push harder and dig deeper. I knew I couldn't rest until Mia was found, safe and sound, and any justice served if someone was responsible for taking her away from those who cared for her. This is how

I thought, which mirrored every officer out tonight. Hope was driving us all.

As I was walking the length of Rosebery Park, the call came in.

"Sergeant, I need you."

# Chapter Nineteen

## Initial evidence

### Jack

As the car rounded the corner to the park entrance, Vikki and Jim were already out of the car, waiting for my arrival. I'd blue-lighted to the pair as best as the car would allow, and fortunately, the roads were clearer than normal. I hoped neither of my team had fallen foul of anything harmful, hence my rapid approach. I pushed that feeling deep down so it didn't get in the way of the quick reactions blue light driving required. The rain had started falling en route and I cursed the heavens as this was not going to help in the search for the missing Mia

It had also rained yesterday too which was a police officer's worst nightmare when hunting for evidence. The water would obscure evidence or worse still, wash it away completely. I grabbed an umbrella from the boot as I got to them, hoping to stop them from getting any wetter than they already may have been. Jim held an evidence bag and wore the telltale blue gloves indicating 'excrements rolled down the hill.' Both officers seemed unhurt though and I was thankful for that small mercy at least.

"Updates. You're both ok, yes?" I inquired, wanting to know both things equally. Vikki smiled at the sentence, appreciating the care I think. It was good to be a great boss as looking after staff was a main priority for me. She was quickly becoming wet through and yet, still managed to smile. Oh, and Jim was also wet. Vikki wore a respectable white top and grey trousers, but the rain was highlighting the strapped vest she wore underneath.

She always pointed out that layers were the best way to stay both warm and covered, yet I quickly averted my eyes still, out of respect for her even though she didn't seem to mind. Was that relish in her eyes? I gave the umbrella to the team and stood in the rain gallantly, but mainly to cool my flushing cheeks.

"Skip, we found a phone, believed to be Mia's. It has a couple of scratches on it, could've been dropped. Some apparent water damage. There's no sign of her though, and a teenager without a phone is not heard of nowadays." (With such deftly reported information, I was back in the room). He was very clearly fearing the worst and now to be fair, so was I. The concern was clear on both their faces at the report, both hoping for the best whilst fearing the worst.

"Book it in and see if there's anything on there that can help. Maybe get our tech guys on the case to check through it for anything evidential. It's all we have currently, so run with it. Also, get her social media channels checked through if they haven't already." I was not one for any of the FaceToks or Instabooks of the world, but young adults loved them, so I crossed my fingers in the hope that there was a jigsaw piece hidden on one of them... I'd take an emoji drawing of an arrow pointing towards anything of note at this point. Jim nodded and moved to their car, glancing at Vikki who hadn't moved.

"Coming Vik?" He said, awaiting an answer.

"I'll help the skipper with a reccy around the park before it's too wet." She smiled at Jim who was grinning. I was oblivious to their unspoken conversation, but they needed morale so hell with whatever it was. Jim handed the brolly to Vikki and left with the bagged phone. Looking back at her, she was beaming up at me offering an elbow. Gingerly I shook it as I was unsure of the gesture. I thought it was for the umbrella as sort of a stand but I think I nailed the correct response.

Which immediately showed me that social skills had once more let me down.

"Come on boss, let's see if we can find her. Other units are on the way as this is a big arsed park. We'll follow the main path as we aren't in uniform in case we see her. Don't want her spooked." She handed me the umbrella and took my arm in hers. I... What? I was generally confused at this point.

"Let's look like a couple in case she's around. Stealth mode!"

"With you now Vik," I clarified, nodding to her to begin the search and we started walking. You may have guessed by now that I'm a little bit on edge around Vik. Vikki. Victoria. Oh God. But what happened next floored me. After a few minutes of searching, she looked up at me and said, quietly and with an obvious undertone;

"You're making me wet."

## Chapter Twenty

### In Holmes we trust.

### Jack

"The umbrella? Move it this way a bit, Skip." She said, following up on her last statement about her dampness level. I was generally confused again. Even to my closeted ears, that seemed quite sexual in nature. Her bodily language even showed signs of arousal too.

I went through the tick list in my head.

⅄ Preening behaviours...

⅄ An open physical posture...

⅄ Leaning in...

⅄ Blushing...

⅄ Prolonged eye contact...

⅄ Wet shirt with two full curvaceous wonders, stacked with joy...

Wait, what the fuck. That last one was certainly not in the handbook.

⅄ The elegant curve of her back beneath the sodden fabric of the shirt...

⅄ Or how she carries herself daily and somehow manages to be both languid and dominant at the same time...

⅄ The deep purr of her voice...

⅄ Or the delicate line of her collarbone, just visible above her neckline...

Fuck, fuck, fuckety fuck.

I rubbed my eyes and looked away, but still felt her against my arm. Get back in the game, Jack.

Splosh.

My foot went into an area of the pathway that seemed lower in density with water than other areas. Just a bit, maybe a millimetre, but enough for my keen senses to notice. It ripped me back to the job as for the briefest of moments I had been distracted. Even with the Vikki issue, I was still on point and could notice awry water levels through a shoe. God, I'm odd.

"This is near to where we found the phone, Jack." There was care in her eyes as she had realised that she hadn't told me the location, yet I had still picked up something. I put my gloves on and quickly placed my hand in the water. Nothing was apparent to the eye, thankfully, except a slight crack in the concrete that the water was seeping into.

There was nothing that I could see so shone a high beam of torchlight around the area.

Again, nothing.

Moving to the bench, I noticed a gouge in the wood which seemed fresh. There were two smaller ones by either side as if caused by a claw of some kind. I noted it for consideration should the evidence lead us in that direction, unsure as to why it would though.

"Should we rope this area off?" Vikki wanted to know.

"We could, but this downpour is going to piss off the scene of crime officer. Let's think. We have a phone. There's no blood on it and some scratch marks. This indicates a high probability that it was dropped. There's no body or blood, although any fluids would, or could have been washed away at this point."

Vikki was listening intently to my train of thought, which was outpouring Sherlock Holmes style with great interest.

"Let's get a marked unit to have another look, maybe get an officer who is search trained. PolSA yes? Police Search Advisor? I'm sure I heard one on accepting the call." She nodded and immediately went to dispatch to request assistance. Even though moments ago, she'd been flirting, (possibly, maybe) she was still one hundred per cent on the case. Professional and beautiful. She was flirting, right? I continued my thought process. (About the case, not Vikki).

"So there's no need for a tent because the ground is sodden. Also, putting up a tent causes community tension and the rumour mill to flow over. Especially when it will literally be covering just the floor." Deep breath and continued my flow.

"OK. No tent, officer with PolSA training to have another look and get the intel team to look into the phone." Satisfied I had the right decision and plan in place, I looked at my watch. 02:15 hrs blinked back at me. We had finished our shift seventeen minutes ago and neither had noticed.

# Chapter Twenty One

## Days into Nights

### Vikki

Vikki hated leaving work for others. It wasn't her at all. She wanted to see cases through to the very end, especially ones with missing people. That was her passion. Reuniting the lost.

She paced the office floor, her frustration palpable with every step. She knew she had to go home and rest as she felt the fatigue of a shift without a break, and the emotional drag on her senses drained her further. The thought of leaving a case for another officer to handle grated against her very being, as she prided herself on her dedication and tenacity, refusing to let any lead slip through the cracks. Yet, as the clock ticked on past the end of shift, the reality of passing the torch gnawed at her conscience. The case was a tangle of nothing leads, each fizzling to nothing and she concluded that she knew it demanded her full attention. But her duty now was to sleep, and rest, although switching off would be all but impossible. With a heavy sigh, she reluctantly briefed her incoming colleague, imparting every detail with painstaking clarity. As she stepped out into the night, a pang of unease settled in her chest, a silent vow echoing in her mind to return and see Mia's safe return. She paused on the steps, contemplating just staying on, even though it was against the skipper's advice.

As this missing person had struck home closer than she'd realised.

At seventeen, (Mia's age), she'd lost her sister, Tessa, to suicide. No one saw it coming, least of all Vikki. Tessa was the life of all the parties they'd both go to. Always the wild one. She was free and alive. She was a vibrant spark that ignited any gathering with her infectious laughter and boundless energy. With her radiant smile and magnetic personality, she effortlessly drew people into her orbit, and they would long to revolve around her. From the outside, Tessa was living her best life, constantly surrounded by friends and the centre of attention in every social setting. Her presence electrified all rooms, and her laughter echoed through the school halls, leaving a trail of warmth and merriment in its wake.

Free and alive.

But beneath the surface lay a different story, one masked by her exuberant facade. Behind her dazzling smile and animated gestures, Tessa carried a burden of pain and sorrow that she hid from the world. Inside, her heart ached with an unspoken struggle of buried emotions, shrouded in the darkness of a secret inner turmoil. Was it the weight of unmet expectations? Or something the family missed? Or just was there, for no reason? Maybe it was the fear of being alone with her thoughts, or the party finally ending that forced her to confront the demons that lurked within the recesses of her mind. Despite this turmoil raging within her, she continued to light up the room with a brightness she forced herself to conjure up. She had an effervescent presence, determined to spread joy and laughter to those around her.

Free and alive.

Whatever the cause, Tessa died long before the police found her hanging from the tree.

At that point, she was free.

In the aftermath of Tessa's death, the morning sun struggled to breach the heavy curtains, casting a solemn hue across Vikki's bedroom. In the suffocating silence, she sat motionless, her mind a turbulent sea of anguish and disbelief. Why? Just, why? The news of her sister's untimely death had shattered her world, leaving behind a void too vast to comprehend. Memories flooded her thoughts like a relentless tide, each one a painful reminder of a life lost too soon. Why, though? She traced the edges of a faded photograph, her sister's smile frozen in time, a bittersweet echo of happier days. In the days that followed, Vikki retreated into herself, her once vibrant spirit dulled by the weight of crushing grief. Her home buzzed with activity, as the family tried to come to terms, each in their very own ways with the loss of Tessa. Vikki was a haze of sorrow. The routine became her lifeline, a fragile thread connecting her to a reality she no longer recognized against the backdrop of her own shattered heart.

Nights stretched into endless hours of solitude, the emptiness of her home, a stark contrast to the chaos of her mind. Sleep eluded her, haunted by dreams of unanswered questions and what-ifs that lingered like spectres in the darkness. She longed for solace, for the comfort of her sister's laughter and the warmth of her embrace, but found only silence echoing back at her. Amidst the numbing haze of grief, Vikki grappled with a whirlwind of emotions, each one a jagged shard of pain tearing at her fragile facade. Anger simmered beneath the surface, a seething resentment towards a world that had failed to save her sister from the depths of despair. Guilt gnawed at her conscience, a relentless tormentor whispering accusations of negligence and inadequacy.

She replayed their last conversation in her mind, searching for signs she might have missed, words left unspoken. Yet amidst the turmoil, a glimmer of resolve flickered within her, a silent promise to honour her sister's memory in every fleeting moment. She sought solace in the quiet corners of her memories, cherishing the laughter and love they had shared, a beacon of light in the darkness. Although the ache of loss would never truly fade, Vikki found solace in the echoes of her sister's presence, a guiding light through the storm.

Vikki decided at that point that she wanted to join the police. To try and find the reason why the Tessa's, the John's, the Simon's, and the Paul's, chose the most ultimate of an end. She'd sat in her thoughts for some time, saying nothing after losing Tessa.

Jack had tried to engage her in conversation before she left and while she loved hearing every word he said, her mood was bleak. She was lost in thoughts past as this case, this Mia, felt closer to home.

They had to finish work, hand it over, and let someone else deal with it. She'd offered to stay on and tried to, but Jack correctly reminded her that they needed sleep to function correctly or they would burn out. He cared clearly about everyone. But recently, she had realised that she loved him.

Truly.

She wanted to be his, to be held in his arms. Supported and to be supportive. Which was weird because he generally wasn't her type. She normally went for the more arty, free thinker in her friend group, but recently, she knew that while they would mildly satisfy her physically, she wasn't with them in mind. Jack, she could talk openly too. About everything, including work. She'd known many officers who couldn't or wouldn't discuss what they'd dealt with on a shift with their partners for fear of scaring them away. Jack knew all this. He'd stay with her, and they could care for each other. Tonight she would tell him as much.

Fuck the consequences.

Fuck Jack. She smiled at the thought and wondered what it would be like. Those two words filled her entire form with a heat she hadn't fully felt before. It was all-encompassing. Being so lost in thought, she hadn't realised that her autopilot had brought her to his car. He was dropping her home to Epsom's outskirts, having been lost in lurid thoughts too sexual to express externally. She knew that Gareth would've appreciated it though, the perv. He was not as polite with his looks, but never stepped over that line to be gross. 'Just a normal old man checking out the rack on a hottie' she thought. Tonight.

'Like right now.' She thought as the clock clicked over to 03:01 hrs.

"Jack. I'm in love with you."

## Chapter Twenty Two

### Honesty is key...

### Jack and Vikki

"Say that again please, Vik?" I replied incredulously, my ordered mind unable to compute the words, let alone the content. I began running through scenarios and conversational threads to try to understand the situation I now faced.

She what? How?

Fear, confusion and something else swept through me, clouding my normally ordered thought process. I mean I loved her too... wait, what? I love her? Where did that come from?

I'd never considered, dreamed even, that someone of her glory could fall for someone as sedate and organised as myself. I had already decided that she could do so much better.

As Vikki's words hung in the air, my heart stumbled, caught off guard by the weight of her confession. For so long, I realised that I was also hiding my feelings behind my mask of professionalism, burying the depth of my emotions beneath layers of stoicism and duty. Yet, at this moment, her declaration pierced through my defences like a beacon of light in the darkness. With each syllable she uttered, I felt the walls around my heart tremble, threatening to crumble under the weight of my hidden desires. The blood-pumping organ seemed to be reaching out for her metaphorically, with unseen arms carving closeness.

No, I must resist it. I must protect her.

As I met her gaze though, I saw in her eyes a reflection of my desperate own longing. A silent echo of the love I'd kept locked away for fear of disrupting the delicate balance of our professional relationship. In this instant, amidst the chaos of the car's interior, I felt a surge of warmth spread through me, thawing the rigid confines of my stoic exterior. With trembling hands, I reached out to her, yearning to bridge the gap between us and express the depth of my affection. In her presence, I found the courage to shed the armour of restraint I've worn for so long, allowing the hidden romance within me to bloom in the light of her love.

I touched her hand; I knew I was lost.

\*\*\*

"I said that I love you. Always have to be honest," Vikki confirmed. She seemed almost relieved, happy even to have said it out loud and flushed as there was no turning back now. Heat filled her at the thought, and it tingled up her spine, a dancing electric shock that pleased her.

Suddenly, she was free.

The sensation felt profound and liberating. She felt a glorious lightness, relief, and a newfound ease, both physically and emotionally. Sitting next to Jack, her heart pounded with a mixture of fear and anticipation, the weight of the confession a heavy weight lifted from her tongue. Ever since she had first met him, she had buried her burgeoning feelings beneath layers of professionalism and duty, guarding them like a most precious secret in the depths of her soul. But now, as she looked briefly into his eyes, she could no longer deny the truth that burned within her. With a voice born of courage and trepidation, she finally spoke the words she'd kept hidden for so long, feeling the weight of their release lift from her shoulders like a burden too long carried. At that moment, she felt a sense of liberation wash over her as if she'd finally cast off the shackles of silence that had bound her for so long. Saying those simple words was stepping into the light after years spent in the shadows, and Vikki found herself enveloped in a sense of relief so profound she felt tears forming in her eyes. She wiped them away, but the happiness and relief remained.

"You love me? Me, yes?" Was all Jack could muster as a vocal response. As the words tumbled into the car, she saw a flicker of surprise in Jack's expression, followed by a warmth that spread across his features like sunlight breaking through storm clouds.

They were yin to yang. Two sides of a coin. Reactions to actions.

* * *

I realised, with her words said, that the feelings I had been quashing were boiling to the surface. I couldn't stop them now even if I wanted to. It wasn't just what we had been through together as officers, it wasn't that we had shared incident experiences together either.

It was a pure destiny. It felt right.

It was however chaotic, and the orderly side of my mind was fighting back with questions which would hamper whatever could be coming.

She was my subordinate. There would be paperwork. Eyebrows would be raised. I struggled to keep the car en route to her home in Epsom as my mind diverted, drawn away by feelings clawing to the surface. I tried to concentrate on what I would say to the Inspector, working through every angle, and considering each answer meticulously. Wait. Why am I preparing this conversation? Am I allowing this to happen? Is this my subconscious falling for her?

I just wanted her to be protected from any fallout.

Wanted her to be safe from everything.

Wanted her.

\*\*\*

Vikki chuckled at Jack's remark, as she somehow expected those exact words, knowing he wouldn't be able to comprehend the relationship change. His vulnerability attracted her more though. He was not one of the standard 'lads' who had tried it on with her before, he was the silent knight, fighting in defence of his lady. He'd always be the one unconsciously kerbside and she had seen this hidden side even though Jack didn't realise he kept it. Looking at him now though, she saw an unleashed fire in his eyes, yet he was fighting a battle of urges over control. Vikki knew he needed orders, he needed her to make the first move.

"Find somewhere." She said quietly, hoping that this was wanted by him as much as the growing feeling deep within her.

She kicked off her shoes and socks into the footwell. He looked down at the action and followed her request without a word, driving down a dark road as she slid out of her jeans. Jack was lost in the only order he had left, the urges within him following her words and actions dutifully. The moonlight seemed to glance and dance on her bare skin. She felt free of the encasing clothing and knew her slender legs were being appreciated from the driver's seat. She chose to continue as they both realised that there was no going back from where they were now. He also wasn't stopping her either. The normal efficiency and demeanour of a police officer were gone now. They'd ended their shift but started something new. She was the object of affection, of lust, of want now and she loved it. Jack watched as her t-shirt was pulled up and over her head causing the mess of yellow-red curls to flow down her skin like a flamed river in sunlight. Vikki sat there as she felt the car's speed increase unconsciously. She began tracing the shards of moonlight with her finger as they caressed her bare skin in the dark of the night.

\*\*\*

I threw the car into a pitch black layby and looked down at her, taking in her curves, her sheer beauty. She was perfect. Utter perfection. The glorious blonde of her hair and the slight redness hidden within was a stark contrast to the alabaster of her skin, unseen in this way before. She writhed and relished my view upon her and her excitement made me feel as if I was already touching her, exploring her bare skin. I heard a voice screaming in the back of my mind, but to hell with control. Fuck reason. She was...

Everything.

I leant the seat back and down as she moved to mount me, easily getting astride me. I wouldn't stop this for anything now. The world around me was gone, disappearing until all I could see, all I could feel, all I could sense, was her.

\*\*\*

As Vikki looked down, she saw that something was missing from behind Jack's eyes and for a moment felt the urgent need to hold him. All of sudden, it was gone as he arched up to kiss her. As their lips met, she melted into him, feeling his clothes against her almost bare form. An electric charge arced and clawed up her back causing her to almost moan into his mouth, such was the feeling. This pent-up, held-back urge was adding to every minute touch. She pushed him back so that she could remove her bra as it was depriving her breasts of his hands. It landed on the seat next to her and she waited, showing herself to him.

\*\*\*

As the bra fell away, I looked up and was immediately lost again in her beauty. This was all I wanted now, all that mattered. I rose in more ways than one, needing to lick the hardened nipple. When I tasted her purity, I raised my fingers to the other. Satiated with their feel, I moved my hand lower, slowly down to her growing moistness and as I felt her wetness, she tasted my mouth, both of us desperately longing to be inside of each other. It was all-encompassing, all-consuming.

\*\*\*

Vikki pushed back, trying to raise herself into a position to remove her knickers, but Jack pulled her back down upon him.

"Wait," he said, almost imperceptibly. He reached into the centre consul of the car, rummaging through various items and pulled out a pair of tuff cut clothing scissors. Vikki flushed as she was shocked at the bold move, thinking she knew what was coming. She arched herself back as Jack slipped the cool metal against her skin, careful for no sharp edges to injure her. Deftly, he snipped at the flimsy material on the left side. It slipped down, partly exposing a shaven bare, and beautiful sex. She smiled as the heat of the moment grew to an almost crescendo. She never expected this from Jack and it was a wild surprise which made her skin static to touch as he slid the scissors against the other side, the only thing holding the last vestige of her clothing in place. With both sides cut, Jack pulled the ruined garment aside. The electric shock of the orgasm filled her unexpectedly. Their sense of connection with each other, their trust, brought this unique feeling of warm liberation. Every millimetre of her was filled with this excited light as he cupped her in his hand while sliding one finger between her lips, feeling her nerves tense and relax, spasming through the sex. Jack waited for her to finish and was pleased that she was happy. His hand now coated in her orgasm. An orgasm created purely by their need for each other.

Vikki then took hold of the scissors.

## Chapter Twenty Three

### Orgasmic...

### Jack and Vikki

Jack felt the cool metal against his skin as Vikki sliced the scissors deftly up his body, shearing his shirt in two. She looked down hungrily, however appreciatively at his slim physique, pleased at the bonus that he looked after himself. She hadn't cared about his body as it was an unknown factor before this moment, but seeing the ridges of his definition was a glorious bounty. It didn't matter to her though, she wanted him for him. As she traced the sinews of the muscles over his stomach, an aftershock snaked up right through her. She was already very wet from the orgasm he had just gifted her, and she wanted more.

She wanted him inside her.

NOW.

Tugging at his trousers, the pair both knew the urgency of the moment and she freed his manhood, grabbing hold of it like a prized trophy. As she did, she positioned herself just above the tip, stalling before entry, after seeing the surprising size of his girth. She started rubbing her wetness along his shaft, readying it for entry. Moaning loudly, unable to control herself, she slid him inside her while his girth stretched her to fit perfectly. Immediately, she felt free and alive, and yet somehow, she was the one enclosed. He couldn't stop himself and was already filling her, not expecting her to feel so good. Vikki held in that position for a brief moment.

Content, filled and happy.

But now she wanted only one thing.

To be fucked.

Hard.

"Wait. Arch your back. I want to hit that spot you like."

The shock of his words waved through her, and she felt the passion in him grow further. To him it was biology offering him a way to please her, to her, it was what she wanted most.

She arched.

She moaned.

And then fell down upon his chest kissing him intently. He picked up on the urgency and began arching himself up into her. Vikki had felt nothing like it before. It was a connection beyond just pleasure, a feeling so encapsulating it was drug-like in its intensity. As Jack responded expertly to her every whim, she wondered if he'd had many previous partners to make him this receptive, but then she realised. He was listening to her, to her body, feeling its need. This was fucking with love attached, a heated need to please her. This was him thinking purely of her pleasure and in turn, getting everything he wanted by default. Jack pulsed up into her, thrusting, whilst securing her, fucking, whilst feeling her. It wasn't long before he too felt the rush of static sexual electricity caress through him, but he held off, wanting to be second to her pleasure. He wanted his manhood coated like his hand was before, glistening from her orgasm. Muscular, powerful legs raised her up, allowing for deeper penetration and further access to her loving wetness.

Vikki came with a force so hard that it racked her form. It jolted right through her, a rhythmic tingle so strong it caught her breath. For moments held in time, all she could feel was the flood of her orgasm and the beat of Jack's heart as her hand, on his chest, tensed .

The moans were very audible in the dark of the night.

Her nails left red marks on his bare chest, but he felt no pain, just her release. Jack gently placed both hands on her hips pulling her down on him. He was so deep within her that he couldn't hold it in anymore, releasing his load at the deepest point of his thrust, filling her with the fluid of his orgasm that Vikki wanted, craved. As their sex ended, they held each other close, still gripped in interlocked sex.

Vikki was held safe in his arms, while she held firm onto his throbbing member, feeling his pulse through it.

Neither wanted to move.

So, neither did.

## Chapter Twenty Four

### 'Hello, Soldier'

### Jack and Vikki

The sun woke us both as it rose in the early minutes of 7 am the next day. When I opened my eyes, it was as if I was back in control, albeit half-naked. In a car. With a woman on top of me. A very naked one.

So, no control whatsoever then.

Neither of us had moved and as Vikki raised herself, she realised we were stuck together. Giggling, she looked down, and I smiled back up at her, appreciating both her company and form.

"I really liked that shirt," I said and Vikki fell about laughing, clinging to me once more.

"I really liked those knickers," she whispered, smiling as the memory of last night played through my mind.

"You are very much a bad influence, young lady," I mock scolded and she feigned a look that she was 'in trouble with the boss.' She wasn't mind you. I had already let her off.

As she fell asleep in the early hours, I had managed to grab a blanket from the back seat to cover her so that she was warm, and her dignity protected. If someone passed though, it would be extremely obvious what we'd been up to, but the thought was there. The car had a stench of sex, so Vikki reached behind her, fumbling to find the keys to start the engine enough to lower the electric window. She immediately regretted it as a cold blast of air rushed in, covering her bare skin with goosebumps.

The sight of her slender form brought a hot flush of blood and before I could 'think of England' the vision of her had brought a hardness rising against her.

"Hello, soldier." She smiled, holding it in one hand. The gentleness of her grasp was exquisite and for the briefest of moments, I thought about having her again, but the light and awake populace made me think against it. If I could feel my legs, I would've kicked myself.

Immediately, I grabbed her for warmth, bringing the blanket tighter around her. 'Yeah right, pull the other one, it dings all the dongs.' I unconsciously said to myself. I wanted her close again; and did not want to ever let her go. To hell with the world, I'll sort that out later. She shivered and was happy to be next to me once again as I was with her. She secured the window once again.

"I know we're rest days, but we really should possibly get dressed, Vik," I said, looking at the remnants of my shirt.

"Yes, Sergeant," she said with a mock salute, jiggling her nakedness to add to the 'carry on' feeling we both had right now. She giggled as she climbed off me, careful not to step on anything important. Like, my bare Sunday roast with trimmings. 'Another saying nailed,' I thought. Her bum did give a quick beep on the steering wheel horn which brought laughter from us both once again.

Now, in the passenger seat, she dressed as best she could but wondered what the hell she was going to do for underwear. She shrugged and pulled on her vest top and jeans, tossing her bra into the backseat.

I felt a little bit sad that I wasn't looking at her nakedness anymore, as she was a sight to behold. I kept thinking 'boobies, boobies, boobies' as I looked at her, wondering why I had reverted to a horny teenager. It was clear though, that she was braless, and I took appraising glances at her. I knew she wouldn't mind, what with all the 'we just did it' and all.

"I've got a change of clothes and wash kit in the boot if that'll help? You can wear my spare pants if you like?" I said hoping my efficiency would impress.

"Why have you got all that?" She proclaimed and then realised who she was talking to. Mr. Prepared for everything. "Oh yes, Captain organised," she continued and shook her head so that I need not worry. She was clearly happy going mercenary or whatever it was called. I got dressed as best I could, having grabbed some bits from my emergency overnight bag. We headed further into Epsom, where Vikki had a little flat, which she shared with her friend.

We were both famished and wanted a copper's breakfast with all the trimmings in a cafe. Wolfing down the food, we kept smiling at each other in a comfortable acceptance that our lives were now forever changed.

"So, this will have to be declared. I must let the governor know." I said quietly to ensure no one could hear and that everyone did not know we were bonking coppers. Vikki knew I was right as always, but chose to leave it hanging, and reached for my hand, holding it and smiling.

"Not today, Sergeant. It's a rest day."

I paid and we left. On the way back to the car she leaned in, walking close to me. It was nice to feel her again.

There was a warm silence on the way back to the car until it was broken by Vikki.

"'We'll work it out," She said, confirming her unspoken train of thought. The conversation in the cafe had clearly been playing on her mind, and she wanted clarification on what they were declaring.

A one-night stand after a traumatic day?

Or something more?

"Vik, we are rest days, and I think you've earned the right to call me Jack. I have seen you naked, remember?" He said playfully, watching as she smiled. She wasn't embarrassed by his words, but she did flush for another reason.

The memory of last night would stay with her for a long time to come, she already knew that, and squeezed his hand lovingly. Their fingers had interwoven as naturally as the sun had risen and Jack hoped this was not a one-time thing, wanting more from her.

She had freed him from the restraints he kept on himself and her wild abandon was so intoxicating.

"Take me home?" Vikki inquired hopefully.

Smiling down at her, they walked back to the car.

The pair spent the day not discussing their burgeoning relationship, almost avoiding it, wanting to experience life through the other's eyes. More sex followed in the late afternoon, but it wasn't as rampant as their first time. There was nothing but tenderness, both had been filled with a longing for the other. They felt love in the hour they spent having sex with each other, they came simultaneously, and often, in an embrace that felt as if the entire length of their bodies were touching, connected.

Vikki drifted off to sleep holding Jack's arm as he held her from behind.

Jack smiled, watching her sleep contentedly.

He moved as close as he could to her and slipped into the embrace of a dream.

# Chapter Twenty Five

## Balls deep on rest day

### Jack and Vikki

The two rest days were anything but. I ached but my God it was worth it. Vik was absolutely an expert at everything. Except for Mario Kart, which she couldn't beat me, due to the fact that I had memorised all the courses for the greatest efficiency. Those bananas were not going to be the death of my green plumber! She even tried putting me off by playing naked, jumping up and down, and everything. It almost worked and only did when she sat on my lap. There was zero chance of Luigi winning when I was balls deep.

You win this time, vagina.

We had the flat to ourselves as her flatmate was working away on a course, so we were barely clothed, which made checking in on work interesting. I tried to keep tabs on all the cases the other teams were dealing with but again, it was very difficult with voracious Vikki around. She was very insistent that we actually had time off, echoing my own supportive words back at me. Breakfast and other meals consisted of quick and easy plates, as it would be too much time away from each other to cook big meals.

"Why are crumpets in packets of nine? Who thought this was a good idea? You eat two at once! There's always a spare one!" Vikki said, thinking way too far into the bread-based conundrum, no one had ever been bothered with before.

"They could package them in a ten, lined up to fit,

like a cylinder." I chimed in, trying to solve the problem Warburtons had caused. "It would be a crumpet column!" I immediately saw the playfulness in her eyes, as she was thinking of another thing that could loosely be described as such. I was happy to oblige but hoped she wouldn't wear it down to a nubbin.

The sex was non-stop constant, and I thought there must actually come a time when she would be full to the brim. Her protein count was definitely through the roof, that was for sure. After two wonderful, sex-filled days, I left to clean up having gone completely through my emergency boot bag.

Happy and smiling, I drove home.

Unaware of the watching eyes.

\*\*\*

In the shadows, wherever the sun created them, the stealthy figure lurked. Its movement is fluid and silent. It was professional in its concealment, having years of hiding behind it. The fur, being as dark as any abyss, helped greatly, with only the silver orbs that were its eyes a giveaway of its presence. The wolf's fur was not the typical russet or brown of its brethren; rather, it was jet black, blending seamlessly with the night itself. Each strand of fur seemed to absorb what little light dared to touch it, rendering the creature nearly invisible in the dim moonlight.

Even in the sun's early light, it was invisible, a master of stealth. As it prowled through the urban landscape, its senses were keen and alert, and it fixed its gaze upon its targeted house. From the outside, the dwelling appeared innocuous, its windows dimly lit from within by the warm glow of light. Rooms would change constantly, from light to dark as the occupiers moved between them. Yet, the wolf knew better than to be deceived by appearances alone.

Humans meant pain. The wolf did not want any to come to them. It would obviously defend itself; but chose to see the humans as something to protect, rather than eat.

Cats and dogs were its choice of food.

With calculated precision, it skirted the perimeter of the property, moving with the grace of a predator on the hunt. Its movements were calculated and deliberate, leaving no trace of its passing save for the faint rustle of street litter beneath its paws.

Though its intentions remained veiled in mystery, one thing was certain. The wolf watched the house with a sense of purpose, its primal instincts driving it forward from the safety of the wooded area it called home.

The occupants remain completely unaware of the silent sentinel that stood vigil outside their door, cloaked in darkness and shadow.

Being on guard for one of the occupants within...

# Chapter Twenty Six

## Mia M.I.A

## Vikki

A few days had passed after Mia's initial disappearance and the team were fearing the worst. Normally something, anything would appear to give the slightest of lifeline. A glimmer of any sort of hope was not showing itself.

Seventeen. Not yet a life fully lived.

As the police teams embarked, trying to find any sign of Mia, the palpable sense of urgency still gripped them. Each member felt the weight of responsibility on their shoulders, and it crushed down. In the service, all officers knew that none of their jobs were 'tick box exercises' as they were dealing with lives. They knew every passing moment could be crucial in finding Mia safe and sound. Mixed emotions swirled. Frustration. Anger. Desperation. All these blended emotions were needed in some form though, as they created the determination to uncover clues, however small. But the biggest driving force was the underlying pressure to bring her home to her worried loved ones. With each step they took, combing through the streets, questioning witnesses, and tirelessly scanning through the meagre evidence, they were fuelled by a shared commitment to do everything within their police powers to reunite Mia with her family. But around each corner, and every door that was knocked upon, nothing was found. Resolves were intensified, as they clung to hope amidst the uncertainty, determined to bring closure to Mia's disappearance.

Vikki looked over at Jack. He was studiously looking

through the gathered evidence to see if there was anything that could be pieced together to help find Mia. She held in a smile, as she watched his incredible mind work through the papers in front of him, remembering the feel of their bodies as one.

They'd talked about what they would say to the inspector about their brief tryst, but they had run out of time due to their continuous need to be naked. They both said that they would transfer if needed; to stay professional. They ended up almost arguing about who would be the one to leave first, so that they could stay together. Being on opposing shifts would be tough, but they both knew that they would make it work. The sacrifice 'argument' had shown they were serious about their joint future. She knew Jack was serious as he wanted her to meet 'Cat.'

Eventually, she had agreed that he would speak to the inspector at the first opportunity and get any paperwork needed to be sorted. This was a new one for them both and guidance from the superior was a must. Her heart sank when Jack had walked to his office, but it was lifted again when he was shooed out. Apparently, there were too many meetings to be had so Jack would try again tomorrow. Vikki smiled inside at them having to wait for an outcome she did not want.

For now, Mia was more important, and Vikki silently worked, trying every angle her deductive mind offered. There was something they had missed, some stone unturned. She leaned back in her chair, a mannerism she'd picked up from Jack, as the soft glow of the desk lamp cast long shadows across the poorly lit room. The lighting strips in the hung ceiling were from the 1980s and seemed to remove light from the large open-plan room. Vikki had been tirelessly combing through the details of Mia's disappearance. Every lead followed, every witness interviewed, yet something continued to elude her and the teams. Frustration gnawed at her, her mind racing as she tried to piece together the puzzle. What was she missing? As she stared at the board covered in photographs and notes, a nagging feeling tugged at her subconscious, a sense that there was a crucial detail she had overlooked. Vikki closed her eyes, mentally retracing her steps, searching for that elusive clue buried within the chaos of the case.

The discovery of the water-damaged mobile phone in the park seemed promising, but its current state only added to her vexation. While the device underwent repairs and downloads, Vikki couldn't shake the feeling of time slipping away. It was their only lead, and she hoped it would crack the case wide open, as it was yielding nothing at the moment. She awaited the phone's retrieval from the forensic repair shop, her mind raced with possibilities and anxieties, knowing that every passing moment could be a crucial timely missed moment in unravelling the mystery before something bad happened to Mia.

And shooting up, she bolted from the room.

* * *

The small door of the first floor was home to the borough's tech nerd, who oversaw all things communicative. Kim was the dictionary definition of a nerd and about ninety percent geek too. She'd been a serving response officer once but after a suspect ran her over in his desperate attempt to flee arrest for cannabis supply, her dreams of working on the frontline had been brought to a crunching stop.

It had taken her months of recuperation and longer still to come to terms with the veered career path. Kim had undergone a whirlwind of emotions and physical sensations after the initial shock. The impact turned to disbelief that the unthinkable had happened, and she fought to get back to the response team. But, as the pain radiated throughout her body with every step, the constant reminder of the danger inherent in the profession, it brought an intense sense of frustration and disappointment, knowing that her ability to serve and protect had been temporarily compromised. This pain moved to a severe sense of vulnerability, grappling with the realisation of her mortality and the fragility of her physical and mental well-being.

Nights would be disturbed by waking panic attacks where her hands would flush cold, and her thoughts would jumble to chaos.

Then a profound resilience followed, and Kim crafted a new version of her former self, using a determination to overcome the setback and return to duty stronger than before. Supported by colleagues and loved ones, she created the unique position of communications officer, dealing with the social media and online presence of the borough. It was relished by the other officers as none would want to venture into the cesspit of police comms.

'We could solve all burglaries, and someone would still complain about something that the post wasn't about' was a regular Kim-ism which she took strength from, hoping to break through to the haters and show the amazing work the front lines were doing for them. It was often a thankless task, but it was her world now. It was something she could do for the troops, so she threw her all into the task.

Vikki opened the door to find Kim talking on one phone and replying online on another. She also had two other screens brightly showing Sky News and the borough's Facebook account. LBC News was also on, with a presenter chattering away about something political. How Kim monitored everything was a mystery to Vikki, who very much could only concentrate on the thing directly in front of her for fear of missing a minute detail.

"Hi…" Vikki opened with a greeting but was silenced with a finger. Kim kept tip-tapping on the phone as her eyes darted between the screens. After a moment, she hung up the phone, put down the other, and muted LBC.

"You said hi. To me? You need me?" She said, her eyes wider and wilder than Vikki thought humanly possible. There was a slightly sweet smell in the air, and she noticed two empty cans of Monster in the rubbish bin beside Kim.

'Explains a lot.' Thought Vikki.

"Yes, Kim. Can you check a social media presence for me? I'll need Twitter, TikTok, Instagram, and Facebook checks, the full works. Anything else you think or can link to our misper Mia too."

And with that, the tech nerd exploded.

# Chapter Twenty Seven

## Gone (a)live

### Vikki

Vikki had never seen fingers work like Kim's. They danced across a keyboard like they were playing a piano concerto in Geek Minor. They were a whizz of speed and efficiency, hunting for information online that the detective had no hope of ever finding. Keys were pressed together on one hand, creating new imaginative quick steps through a waltz of dancing information. Immersed in the glow of the multiple screens, Kim delved into the depths of social media with a fervent determination blazing like wildfire, unstoppable and all-consuming, igniting every corner of her being with an unyielding intensity. Her fingertips flashed across the keyboard in search of a digital treasure trove and with the keen eye for detail she was renowned for, the hunt was afoot. Kim's arsenal of search algorithms navigated through a labyrinth of tweets, posts, and updates, her gaze fixed and unfaltering in the electronic glare. Each click and scroll hopefully brought her closer to the missing puzzle piece of evidence needed, as she sifted through the myriad of hashtags, location links, and timestamps, piecing together the virtual breadcrumbs scattered across the digital landscape. A digital area search without any boot leather on the ground.

With a sudden flurry of activity, Kim ticked off platforms as she worked and leaned back on her chair, visibly relishing the thrill of the hunt and the possible satisfaction of a successful digital expedition. Snapchats and TikToks flew past the screen, as comment sections were checked, and posts investigated for any relevant updates. Accounts were cross-referenced across the differing platforms to see if there were repeat commenters. Kim ensured to leave nothing left unseen.

"Nothing, Mia is still M.I.A from all those platforms," Kim reported. "Unless she's using a ghost account or a friend's one, but I don't see the point in that outwardly. Maybe for DMing someone? If so, that's a needle in a big-arsed universal haystack."

"What about Facebook? Twitter? Instagram? Anything there?" Vikki wanted to know, trying to use what little knowledge of social media she had.

"Ok so, she hasn't got a Facebook account because she's not forty, Twitter is now called X and I'm checking her Insta next." Kim explained as if this would be common knowledge. She thoroughly enjoyed being of use to the detective constable and her fingers began the technical dance of the nerds once more.

Kim stopped almost immediately.

She had a look of confusion filling her features and Vikki craned to look at her screen.

A video was playing a repeat of Mia being knocked out of the camera shot.

All that could be seen was a flash of white fur.

## Chapter Twenty Eight

### Friday Bathtimes

### The Watcher

After the girl became dinner, it took multiple attempts to bathe the white wolf, as he was covered in the scarlet blood of his last meal.

Cleaning a wolf of blood in a bathtub was akin to wrestling with a reluctant beast in a marsh of molasses thought the struggling Nathan, but it was a task much needed. The wolf, grumpy yet content after its meal, begrudgingly submitted to the cleansing process, happy to have clean fur. It was sticky with congealed blood, clinging stubbornly, and required relentless scrubbing to dislodge the crimson remnants. Despite the wolf's occasional protests, woofs of disapproval and impatient grumbles, there was a flicker of contentment in its eyes, a silent acknowledgement of the necessity of the task.

Soap bubbles mingled with the viscous residue and the wolf's demeanour softened slightly. White found a strange satisfaction in this ritual of purification, amidst the discomfort of sticky blood and confined quarters. The wolf sat down in the bathtub with an audible, squelching thud, accompanied by a gruff of thanks to his cleaner.

His dinner would hold its hunger over for now, but it would soon return. Another meal would need to be found. Steaks from Farm Foods weren't enough, dry food for the voracious, but it was all they had. Killing the girl, while fun and filling, would have raised awareness that a killer was in the humans midst. They hated that and would quickly turn on each other to find the culprit.

Some would blame people they feared, or people they hated, but in this instance, they'd never guess Nathan and White were the killers. Household pets were the next food of choice but even they brought unwanted awareness. Humans loved their pets and despised them being eaten.

'Were they even killers though?' Thought Nathan poignantly. The farmer is not a killer when he culls his herd for the slaughterhouse. This is just the same. He knew it was a way of justifying their actions, a way of easing the quiet whisper of his conscience. Another hunt would help ease it. He sneered as he washed the mighty beast down.

He felt the muscular definition under the thick snowy mane and felt arousal at the contact. It was tantamount to touching himself and gave the same initial tingle inside him.

Another kill.

Nathan smiled and rubbed the large beast between the ears as the last of Mia was washed away.

# Chapter Twenty Nine

## MIAsma of despair

### Vikki

Vikki stared at the image for what seemed like too long, especially as there was another person in the room. 'What the hell is that?' ran through her thoughts as panic welled within her. Vikki felt the blood drain from her extremities and a tightness filled her. The feeling of dread filled her mind and gave her a crushing internal clamp in her heart.

Is this now a kidnapping?

A murder?

What had happened to Mia?

Neither of the occupants of the small room had uttered a word for a minute now and the silence was broken by Kim moving uncomfortably in her chair.

"I... That... I don't know," was all she could bring to the impossible conversations Vikki's team were about to have. The video was clear, Mia was talking into the lens, and then she wasn't. There was no sound to the film and seemed to be clipped badly, reposted by an account in the name of Gary_2002 and tagged with Mia's own Instagram username. His comment below simply read 'WTF??'

All that was clear to Vikki now was the snow white of the fur, and that she needed to tell Jack.

"Download that and get me the best still photo you can, please. Email it through. Thanks Kim." Without confirmation, she left the room, heading back to her team with this new, nonetheless confusing news. In all her years as a police officer and then detective, she had never seen anything like this. She felt a surge of perplexity coursing through her veins as she watched the second of footage on the screen, her brow furrowing with intense confusion. The video depicted something surreal—a merest glimpse of a white-furred... thing. Its form was indistinct, its movements both eerie and otherworldly. It had to be a dog.

There was no other rational choice. She was known for her rationality and keen investigative skills yet found herself grappling with a maelstrom of conflicting emotions—doubt, disbelief, and a nagging sense of curiosity. How could such a thing exist within the confines of her understanding? 'Stop it, Vik.' She chided, trying to bring her thoughts back to normalcy. Yet, the undeniable evidence stared back at her from the screen, challenging her perceptions and stirring a primal unease deep within her psyche. With a determined resolve born from years of unravelling mysteries, Vikki knew that she couldn't ignore this enigma. It was the only lead the team had at this point.

She would delve into the shadows, confront the unknown, and seek the truth lurking behind the veil of confusion because Mia needed her to.

\*\*\*

"I can't believe what I'm seeing here Vik." Said Gareth and Jim followed with his incredulity as well. Vikki looked over at Jack who was also studying the image, a sullen look on his face. It was an expression she had never seen on the man she'd fallen for. There was obvious concern, but a hint of something else. Something deeper.

"There was that weird call a couple of years ago on your old patch when the family knocked on the station door claiming they'd seen a big wolf or something. But obviously, when we checked into it, it was clearly bollocks. Wolves in Surrey? Shit." Gareth said, leaning over Vikki a little too close for her comfort.

"Dunno if it was white-furred though, think it was grey. Or black. Lemme check and see..."

And with that, he opened the shared intelligence report from 2022.

Written by Metropolitan Police Constable Alex Chambers.

# Chapter Thirty

## Good times / Bad times

### 2022

"Dad, a hotdog is basically a sandwich, yes? Or is it a sausage roll?"

The words of Ava, the six-year-old child looking quizzically up at her father initially threw John into a spin, unable to compute both the logic and reason behind the sentence. She munched on the German festive snack and left the image hanging having moved on from the sentence, distracted by a myriad of shiny baubles.

But it plagued her father for the next hour. She was both right and incredibly wrong. Ava tended to state such things, much like the legendary 'Cheese is just a loaf of milk' which baffled both her parents for months.

As the pair walked through the Christmas market of Kingston Town Centre they saw the buzz of merriment, awash with green and red tat to sell to the festive families. Each year the Xmas excitement regrew as people came back to a normal reality after being imprisoned in their homes due to the recent COVID-19 pandemic. It was becoming a distant but remembered memory of years past, but as 2022 came to a close, the thought of more lockdowns was a complete impossibility. And so, the markets opened for their handcrafted wares once more, much to the delight of Ava. It was the same every December. She would step out into the chilly December air, barely able to contain her excitement. Her breath puffed out in little clouds as she tugged her woolly hat down over her ears and pulled her mittens tighter. The air was filled with the sound of laughter, Christmas carols, and the delicious smell of festive treats. The first thing Ava noticed was the giant Christmas tree in the middle of the market square, sparkling with thousands of twinkling lights and colourful ornaments. It was the biggest tree she had ever seen, (since last year), and she marvelled at the way it seemed to touch the sky. Surrounding the tree were dozens of wooden stalls, each decorated with garlands and fairy lights, creating a magical glow.

Her eyes widened as she passed a stall selling all sorts of sweets and treats. There were candy canes as tall as her arm, gingerbread men with icing smiles, and shiny toffees wrapped in bright foil. She could already taste the sugary sweetness just by looking at them. Next to it was a hot chocolate stand, and the rich, warm scent of cocoa wafted through the air. She could see the marshmallows floating on top of the steaming mugs, and she knew she had to have one. Further along, Ava's attention was caught by a stall filled with handmade toys and crafts. There were knitted teddy bears, wooden trains, and delicate ornaments painted in festive colours. An old man with a kind smile was carving something out of wood, and she watched in fascination as the shape of a reindeer began to emerge from the block.

The sound of jingle bells drew her attention towards a small stage where a group of children were performing Christmas carols. Their voices blended beautifully, singing familiar songs like 'Jingle Bells' and 'Silent Night' and Ava joined in quietly, her heart swelling with the spirit of the season.

As the evening grew darker, the market lights seemed to shine even brighter. Ava's dad lifted her high enough to see over the crowds, and she felt like she was on top of the world. She could see the entire market from up there – the twinkling lights, the happy faces, and the beautiful decorations. It was like stepping into a Christmas fairy tale. With her heart full and her hands warm in her mittens, Ava knew this was a Christmas she would never forget. The Kingston Christmas market was a place of wonder and joy, where every corner held a new surprise and every moment was filled with magic.

John though was never one to fall for the cash-grabbing festivities, but with a six-year-old daughter, you had to use your 'ima-gin-a-tion' as she would say. The pair continued through the lights and sounds of the mid-December hubbub smiling and enjoying themselves as all the different scents of the season assailed them. But time had crept up on them, and they walked slowly back to the Rose car park where their carriage home awaited. Both hated the walk as they had filled their bellies with all the tempting treats, Ava still full from the sausage dog 'rollwich' from earlier.

As they passed Kingston Police Station, a well-wrapped-up policeman nodded hello to them both, filling his face with a welcoming smile.

"Hope you had a great night?" he said with a warmth the night did not have.

"Yes, I ate a sausage roll!" came the reply from Ava.

PC Alex Chambers nodded goodbye and entered the clinically aged building, eager for his next tea and biscuit.

Again though, John was in a spin of sausage-based 'ima-gin-a-tion.'

It didn't last long though as the pair were assailed with a new collection of smells, urine being the acrid winner.

They paid for parking quickly and found their car with haste as Ava was bundled inside. The small child was bundled into the vehicle with the care and attention of a careful parent, but also with just enough urgency to sort the myriads of straps and buckles the seat required. John closed the door with a sudden sense that he was being watched. This was picked up by Ava who tried to manoeuvre herself around to see what her father was looking at. She was held in place by the security of the seatbelt, so her view was restricted, barely boosted by the pillow she loved sitting on. John scanned the car park, which was well overdue for a maintenance overhaul as strip lights blinked their last gasps of brilliance.

In between two parked cars was a shape that was mostly concealed in shadow. It was larger than the size of an average dog, but it was lower and lither, its sinewy form athletic, but wary. The lights of the car park glinted off its dazzling eyes which were completely silver and danced like fluid metal in an organic orb. The silver was tinged with a green that was reminiscent of the Christmas trees the pair had recently viewed. However, this hue added a touch of nature to the fur covering the rest of the form.

Moving out from the shadows, John could see the fur to be grey, coarse and dirty, covered in woodland detritus. Mud smeared along one flank told the story of a creature sleeping outside, under the stars. It was a coat tainted by the earthy hues of mud and dirt, its once sleek fur now bearing the marks of a rugged existence, each strand intertwined with the remnants of its wild pursuits.

Even through the muck, the creature seemed new and mythical. Enticing to touch almost.

The creature seemed inquisitive, almost playfully energetic as it bounded from roof to roof, the talons on its feet click-clacking on the metal. It seemed to be listening to the sound, curious and inquiring. Its claws and teeth, though sharp, carried a subtle luminosity, contributing to the overall enchanting aura of this unique and imaginative creature.

As the inquisitive Ava tried to look at what her father was staring at from within the car, the charm and wonder of the creature dwindled for her father as it pounced.

# Chapter Thirty One

## From Black to light

### 2022

Amidst the flickering glow of distant streetlights, the black-furred wolf reluctantly stepped into the urban jungle it had avoided for so long.

Because the Grey one was making a move.

It could not let more be killed. Black had to take down the older beast. It had to intervene as it was driven by the need to save lives. The Grey was hungry and driven by its stomach to hunt.

For years it had lived in the shadows, its jet-black fur a boon to stealth. For sustenance, it mainly stuck to eating small wild animals. When hunger drove him, he'd risk a suburban cat. He hated doing that though as it knew it brought pain to the human owner.

As recompense, Black thought to leave the head of the pet near the home so that the owner at least had finality and wasn't left longing for a cat that would never return. It was a macabre choice, but Black knew truth over mystery was always better closure. The dark wolf returned its attention to Grey who was prowling, stealthily through a desolate car park. Both of their keen senses were heightened by the moonlit night. Black was younger and more able to hide knowing that Grey was oblivious to his presence.

An unusual tension hung in the air as the reluctant hunter pursued its quarry, another wolf whose fate seemed intertwined with his own through the shadows. The echoes of the urban jungle resonated as the onyx predator hesitated, torn between its innate instincts to be invisible and an internal struggle to save lives in danger. Black found himself reluctantly cast into the role of a lone pursuer, and the car park, usually a haven for vehicles, could become an unconventional battleground where the hunter and the hunted engaged. Each step taken was laid with a heavy reluctance, but as Grey moved, Black sensed that it had found a target.

The man and the small girl walked ever closer to their impending death which stalked them both.

Black knew that its time in the shadows was at an end.

It moved towards the hunter as it moved towards its prey.

# Chapter Thirty Two

## Death comes calling

### 2022

The barred teeth were wet with spittle as they streaked towards John's face, intent on tearing into the soft tissues found there. He managed a brief whimper as the beast's leap drew it ever closer. Ava's mouth was agape, unsure what was happening, but scared into a terrified silence. To the small girl, the events were incomprehensible, her memories unable to draw on little to make sense of what was happening.

John, however, knew pain and possibly even death was incoming.

He wasn't ready.

Who would protect Ava from these teeth?

He closed his eyes and in one swift brave move, locked the car door in the hope that he would be the only one to feel the pain of the animal's ferocity.

In the darkness of his protected vision, no pain came.

Death did not knock.

Suddenly, John heard the thud of a forceful blow and an accompanying yelp of surprise. It was followed by a deep, guttural growl which was a clear threat in nature.

The fierce noise had started low to the ground and then rose till it was above his height.

He risked opening an eye.

Then the other.

Encompassing his vision was a mass of black fur,

standing six feet tall. He could only see the back of the creature as it had positioned itself between John and the grey creature that had wanted to harm him. It was his turn to be unable to process the scene. Unable to move, he watched the first wolf-like thing growl up at the second, darker-furred animal, its attention now solely focused on its surprise attacker. John felt that to the grey wolf, he was no longer a target, no longer even there, such was the intent of its gaze on the new beast.

Again, it pounced, but the black wolf was ready.

Moving with incredible speed, the larger, darker wolf twisted, allowing the grey one to fly past it, only to be caught in a pawed grip. It caught the smaller entity mid-flight, slamming it violently to the ground. There was a sickening thud of bone against concrete and blood streaked outward from the impact point. The large beast went down to all fours, pushing its mass against the smaller captive, but with flight born of desperation, it lashed out against the darker assailant. It roared with pain as wolf-clawed paws ripped into the side of the dark beast above it. Dark fluid sprayed from the wound covering the car to the left, and some towards John, who was still motionless. Knowing there was fight still in the beast below, a roar filled the air from the black-furred wolf, and it opened its mouth in threat. As John watched, in one smooth movement, it chomped down on the grey-furred wolf below, encompassing most of its snout and face in its mouth.

Teeth tore through skin and bone, rendering the fight over almost immediately.

Moving back from the creature, the black wolf watched as the grey beast dissolved right in front of it, leaving the remaining three to watch as it became a viscous scarlet puddle of blood and gore. It died leaving little of what it was, just a smear of red on the car park floor, which was already losing its blooded colour.

John looked over at his saviour as it crunched through what it had bitten off. Blood and bone particles splattered its dark fur as it chewed, and John's legs gave out. He passed out leaving a nightmare in front of him.

\*\*\*

The beast finished eating and moved to John's side.

As it passed, it took an inquisitorial lick at the puddle and then looked down at the fallen father. The fluid had become darker, losing the rich redness of blood, and was now an almost black, inky stain on the floor. The car door where blood was splattered had lost its viscosity and dripped mostly away too. Black watched as it slowly fizzled and began disappearing leaving little evidence of the wolf it once was.

'Was this to be his fate too?' thought the large muscular beast. From his new position, he heard the whimper of Ava from behind the window near him. Although scared, she began opening the rear window. She left a small enough space to talk through but not enough for the wolf to gain access.

"Don't eat my daddy." Ava said, terrified but driven to protect her father. Black raised itself to look at her fully and placed its large, clawed hand between the gap created by the window's descent. The weight of the massive beast brought the glass crunching downward, and it was driven forcefully into the door frame. Ava whimpered as the wolf's snout entered the car. It sniffed her and then lowered its head to show that it wasn't a threat to both her, or her father. Large claws gripped the side of the car, but the young child, in both fear and wonder, reached out tentatively, touching the head of the beast that had saved them. The only thought she'd had was to protect her daddy, but now she was driven to thank this thing, no matter how monstrous it was. Her hand was immediately lost in the dense fur, which had appeared coarse and weather-worn when she had first seen it, but now… It felt exactly the same as human hair. As she moved her hand, one of the long ears twitched uncontrollably as if it was feeling tenderness for the first time and it was triggering a lost nerve.

Looking into each other's eyes, the beast nodded slightly to the small girl, it gently licked her nose, and then bounded off, into the night.

## Chapter Thirty Three

### Wolves... Fucking two of them

#### 2022

"I tell you it was a fucking wolf! Two of the fucking things!" John's anger overflowed as he hugged Ava to his side. It was an embrace that was as much for him as it was for her because knowing his child was safe was all that mattered. He'd run back to the police station as soon as his consciousness allowed, carrying his little girl in his arms more out of relief than to expedite their progress.

How they were both alive after the wolves fought in front of them would forever be a mystery to the older man, alongside how his child was so calm. She'd been sitting next to him when he awoke, with a hand on his chest, completely unharmed.

Not even a tear had streaked down her face.

Now, within the safety of the front counter, locked inside the reporting booth, he'd tried to explain what had happened to the pair moments before. Speaking through the terror they faced, he explained that it was not a dog, or a fox, but a 'fucking wolf!'

"Sir, please calm down, you're safe here and we will assist, but I'm sure you can imagine how this all sounds. We want to help, but wolves with silver eyes?" The Public Access Officer was indeed trying to help but the incredulity of the details was hard to accept.

PAO Chloe Langstone, continued to try and calm him down. Ensuring to smooth out her scouse accent while lowering the tone, even though the story seemed an absolute impossibility. John was having none of it though still reeling from the encounter they'd been through. As he continued, a police officer rounded the corner, into the rear of the booth. He had a mug of tea in his hands and was eagerly dunking a chocolate hobnob dangerously low within the beverage.

He smiled down at the young girl and said, "Well hot dog, we meet again!" It was a clear effort to remove some of the tension in the small room, and it worked on the young child who waved eagerly back at him.

"Hi again, Mr Officer." She chirped.

"You can call me Alex. But everyone else must call me PC Alex," he said, winking at her. "Dad, can I ask... sorry, let me guess, Ava? That's your name, right?"

She looked incredulously back at him, at the incredible detective work this police officer had shown. Genuinely delighted, she nodded enthusiastically, not realising the names were written on a notepad in front of Langstone.

"Ava, firstly you're both ok. That's the main thing. Can you tell me what happened though, because I'd love to hear it?" Alex sat in a chair opposite her, placing his tea in front of him, eager to hear her retelling as it was a tool for both reassurance and it was also good to get an unadulterated view.

Ava did not hold back.

Enthralled, Alex noted the details and asked Langstone to email him all the information she had taken down for further investigation.

"Sir, I think I have everything from you both and it seems like you need to get this little one home. I'll walk over with you to your car and have a look around if that'll help?" Alex said reassuringly and it was eagerly accepted by the worried parent, who was feeling the calming effects of the police officer's actions. He knew full well it was to defuse the situation but he appreciated the efforts he was going through to assist.

Leaving the station John walked, holding his daughter's hand. He noted that she was also holding Alex's and skipping merrily between the older men. The sight of her brought his strength back, his courage borne of her safety.

"Thank you for doing this, officer," John said as they neared the car park.

"Some would say 'it's our duty' or something like that, but I always consider what we leave behind. It's about paying it forward, isn't it?" Alex smiled warmly at John, knowing that he'd helped.

'Tick, money earned,' thought Alex proudly.

The car park was oddly silent for the busy time of year, and they made it to John's car without seeing anyone or more to the point, any stray wolves.

"There should be a body or something just at the end, near the boot," John said, a clear note of worry in his voice as he furtively looked around.

Stepping in front, Alex walked between the two cars to where his victim had reported.

No body, parts or even blood could be seen.

What was left though was an inky stain, which shimmered slightly like spilt oil. The purple and green glinted iridescently as the thin sheen moved in a play of colours, almost rainbow in effect. John looked incredulously at it as no words of explanation would suffice.

Ava walked to the police officer's side and tugged at his hand once more. Alex knelt to be on the same level as the small child as she whispered,

"The good wolf saved us."

# Chapter Thirty Four

## Historic leads

### 2024

"See! I told you. Bollocks." Gareth explained as he shut the report down. Internally, he'd hoped that it would lead to something, anything that could help the team as he was becoming more and more aware that he wasn't contributing as much as he'd like.

"It says that PC Alex had to leave them as there was a collapse in the street around the corner near the Rose Theatre. Apparently, some old guy was just standing near the car park and then collapsed stone-cold dead. Was not linked apparently." He added.

Vikki looked back at the white-furred still photo capture and realised that reading the previous report had not helped at all. She felt more uneasy now than before Gareth's additional evidence.

'So, a white, grey, and / or a black wolf is running around our streets? Why hasn't anyone seen it or them?' She wanted to know the answer more than anything now, but her attention was drawn to Jack. He'd remained silent throughout. This was not like him at all, as he would almost always verbalise his reasoning out loud in a 'thought dump' to help clarify the evidence at hand. It was amazing to see the cogs audibly spoken and a learning tool for any in earshot.

Turning, he walked back to his desk without a word.

\*\*\*

I don't know why it affected me so much. It was an

image from deep down, but one I could not put my finger on. This couldn't be another aberration like the mystery of Alex's death one year earlier. I don't know if my logical mind could take another one.

I needed the scientific answer to everything. There was a reason for it all, there had to be. Otherwise, where were we as a human race? We'd descend into chaos and anarchy and it would rule the streets. Police are the first bastion to that disorder and when incidents could not be explained, I felt that this bedlam was one step closer. Was humanity on the verge of a chaotic oblivion? Was I being too dramatic? Whatever though, I knew that I had to stop this.

I caught Vikki's eye, and she was looking over at me with concern in her eyes. It was subtle but I knew her better than anyone.

It was a concern brought by care. By love.

We are closer now.

I've let her in.

And I must protect her from this possible pandemonium.

I must keep the wolves at bay.

# Chapter Thirty Five

## Mia still M.I.A

## Jack

"What do you mean it's not a murder?" I said, almost annoyed with the Murder Investigation Team sergeant. He'd said that there was no body and just a flash of something on a social media feed which wasn't enough to go on yet. He was right mind you. It wasn't. Mia was still missing and there was no evidence to push it higher up the ranks and get more boots on the ground. Everyone was on it, even in passing. Safer Neighbourhoods Teams on patrol were on the lookout, as were Response and the Proactive CID cars.

Missing.

Presumed...?

This one was annoying me. More so than usual. There was something I was missing, something nagging in the back of my mind that I hadn't fit into the puzzle. As I sat at my desk, the weight of the unsolved case pressed heavily on my mind. Mia, a young woman with dreams and aspirations, vanished without a trace days ago. Despite countless hours spent combing through evidence and chasing leads, the truth remained elusive. Each passing day deepened my sense of frustration, and an urgency was gnawing at my soul. What happened to Mia? Was she abducted, or did she vanish of her own accord? The possibilities taunted me, mocking my inability to provide even the simplest of answers to her distraught family. Every photograph of her plastered across the city streets felt like a silent accusation, a reminder of my failure to bring her home.

Yet, amidst the darkness of uncertainty, a flicker of determination ignited within. I wouldn't, couldn't, rest until I had unravelled the mystery shrouding Mia's disappearance. I needed to bring closure to those who clung to hope in the face of despair. Of possible grief. All the talk of wolves though... Looking around the room, I realised that there had been a shift change and I was looking out at the faces of the next team on shift. In my thoughts, I had dismissed them on autopilot. I hoped Vikki was ok and wondered what she must think of me. I gathered my things and left for the day, getting to my car about thirty minutes later. My thoughts were awash with reasoning and still, I failed Mia. Getting in the car I flicked on the radio to hear the news report on LBC chime in.

"Missing girl Mia, 16, is still being sought by local officers. She is described as..." I flicked the switch off. I didn't need to hear the press lines that I'd authorised or be reminded of the fact that she was still out there. I needed a run. I needed to be in the silence of my own mind, to hopefully clear it. I pulled into a parking space and checked on the restrictions, luckily finding them ping up on Ringo that it was free. I always kept a spare kit in my boot for emergencies, alongside an overnight bag in case we were kept on at work. I'd had to refresh it recently, which brought back fond memories. The differing bags were over the top, but better to be prepared than not.

Costa was still open, and I entered, wanting water to quench a thirst I was intending to create. It was a pretence of politeness too as I needed their loo to change. As I laced up my running shoes, I tried not to notice the graffiti offering sexy time as it was the furthest thing from my mind at that minute, although I would have appreciated the security Vikki's embrace brought. I might be a sergeant, but I'm lost in the body heat of the one I love. It felt good to admit it once again to myself. I thought, I should tell her whenever I can.

The weight of the day felt like a storm cloud pressing down on me though, heavy and relentless. I know I shouldn't, but I take it home with me, policing isn't just any job. Much the same as the NHS or Firefighters. Mental images tended to linger like a bad meal, popping up at the most inopportune moment. As soon as I stepped back outside, a gentle breeze of anticipation swept over me. I took a deep breath, inhaled the crisp, evening air, and began to run.

And.. I'm gone, lost in the moment.

The first few strides are like wading through a thick, tangled forest, each step an effort to push through the brambles of my stress and fatigue. But soon, as my pace steadies, I found my perfect rhythm, and the world around me starts to blur. I become like a river, flowing steadily downstream, carving my path through the landscape. It doesn't even matter where I run either. It was just to be out running. The pounding of my feet on the pavement was a steady drumbeat, a call to the wilds within me. Each breath I took was like a gust of wind through the trees, refreshing and invigorating. My worries began to fall away, like leaves drifting from the branches in autumn, leaving me lighter with each passing moment. As I ran, I felt the energy of the earth beneath me, grounding me and pushing me onward. My thoughts scatter like a flock of birds taking flight, leaving my mind clear and free. I am the deer bounding through the meadow, swift and sure, each stride a celebration of my freedom. The sun had dipped below the horizon, painting the sky in hues of orange and pink, and I felt a sense of peace washing over me, like the calm after a huge devastating storm. I am alone in my journey, yet I feel connected to everything around me—the rustling leaves, the chirping crickets, the distant hum of life beyond the trail. I now had the chance to focus, to refocus my thoughts, so that they could align to order. This was the only time I felt so close to nature, as its wilderness always seemed too chaotic. Getting back to the car, I drove in silence, calm and awake once again. Yet, before I could realise what I had done, I had subconsciously not driven home.

\*\*\*

The runner's breath came in ragged gasps as he sprinted through the wooded park, his pounding footsteps echoing against the silent, looming trees. Cloaked in the unseen shadows, the wolf stalked him, its silver eyes gleaming with predatory focus. Each leap and bound through the underbrush was effortless, every move calculated, keeping pace with the man's frantic dash.

Hidden by the thick undergrowth, the wolf's presence was felt more than seen, a haunting whisper of danger in the rustling leaves and the nearly imperceptible crunch of twigs underfoot.

The man glanced over his shoulder, his heart pounding with the exertion, but saw nothing other than the dense, dark wilderness, as the unseen predator kept pace easily with the lone human.

## Chapter Thirty Six

### #MondayMeowtivation

### Cat

'Miaow' thought Cat as he sat next to his empty food bowl. The magic box had yet to feed Cat, and he yelled loudly in dispute. It was food time, and the two legs knew this. He wasn't home yet, and Cat's bowl was empty. Cat knew it dispensed crunchy goodness when his pet had not returned home but it was too early for the machine thing to click into life.

Rudeness.

Turning, Cat licked a paw and decided to prowl through the familiar areas of Epsom it knew so well. He wiggled through the cat flap and stood triumphantly in the 'out' side of the door. This was his land; he'd made sure of it by rubbing himself against everything and all he surveyed was still his. He could smell himself on everything. Cat's tail flicked lazily behind him as he sauntered around to the alley. The late afternoon sun cast warm rays down upon his fur. It dappled the floor with golden hues as Cat sauntered past an old dustbin. This was not his yet, so he made sure to make it so. Rubbing his face against it, he knew that that metal object was now indeed his.

'Miaow' he thought triumphantly.

Cat's senses tingled with the comforting scent of the streets and the familiar odour of his human pet and the lingering aroma of the treats he bestowed upon Cat was picked up by his keen senses. He had failed that day though, and Cat decided to make sure to shit just to the left of his litterbox as a lesson to his pet. Maybe even piss scent a single shoe.

Today, something was amiss. A scent foreign yet strangely alluring hung in the air, weaving its way into his whiskers and stirring a primal curiosity within. Cat's ears pricked forward, following the scent trail, cautious steps leading him towards where the aroma lay.

There, in the dimly lit alleyway, stood a figure unlike any it had encountered before. A massive black wolf, its fur as dark as the night sky, its eyes gleaming with a wisdom beyond Cat's understanding. He froze in his tracks, its fur bristling with a mix of fear and fascination.

"Hiss, Hiss! Maaorrao!" Cat said defiantly with as much intimidation as he could muster. The wolf regarded the smaller animal with a steady gaze, its nostrils flaring as it inhaled the cat's scent with a knowing air. Cat could feel the wolf looming over it, a silent sentinel in the midst of its presence.

Despite Cat's instincts urging him to flee, he held his ground, mesmerised by the enigmatic creature before him. There was no malice in its gaze, only a sense of quiet understanding, a recognition of the bond that transcended the boundaries of their species. Tentatively, Cat took a step forward, closing the distance between them. The wolf inclined its head in acknowledgement, a silent invitation to explore this strange connection between the two. As they stood there, two creatures, from different worlds, a silent understanding passed between them.

There was no threat from either.

In that moment, Cat knew that this encounter was

no mere chance occurrence—it was a glimpse into the mysteries of the universe, a reminder that beneath our differences lay a shared kinship, bound by the threads of existence itself.

"Miaow," he said in confirmation.

Cat weaved between the wolf's legs, scent marking his familiarity as the wolf bent its head down and opened its mouth.

The large tongue moved roughly along Cat's head, leaving a wet trail down to his shoulders.

"Miaow," Cat said thoughtfully wondering why the big thing hadn't finished with his bath. With a final nod of farewell, the wolf turned and melted back into the shadows, leaving the smaller animal standing alone in the alleyway, its heart pounding with a newfound sense of wonder.

It was at that moment that Cat decided to clean himself properly.

***

Black left the small animal alone even though it had originally intended to eat it. It would have to find another meal tonight as this animal felt important somehow. It had a 'safe' smell.

How Black knew this was beyond him, but this small animal had to be protected as if it were his own.

## Chapter Thirty Seven

### Do one

### Leigh

Leigh had had a shit of a day.

Firstly, the local coffee shop had fucked up her name, and her oat milk chai latte.

'How the fuck do you mess up Leigh?' she thought angrily, remembering seeing 'Lee' scrawled on her cup. Did she look like a geezer bloke? One hundred percent not. Then, the local Greggs had run out of their world-famous sausage rolls. A treat which she granted herself once a month, and there was no way she was eating one of their vegan options. 'They were meant to be 'alternatives' but by fuck, they weren't,' thought Leigh.

It was borderline an apocalypse by lunch.

Clive, the kitchen manager, was being a letch again with all the girls on bar duty making them all feel like they needed a shower. For a week. In acid. And they'd still feel just as dirty after.

His lines ranged from,

"Do you work for the post office? I thought I saw you checking out my package!" to "I'm a bird watcher and I'm looking for a Big Breasted Bed Thrasher. Have you seen one around here? Failing that, I'll be on the lookout for a nice couple of tits."

After each one, he'd laugh throatily but secretly be seeing if there was a glimmer of acknowledgement from his intended target. He'd take any sort of buying sign.

There never was.

The vomit-inducing sexual harassment continued into the afternoon, going unheard by the bar manager who couldn't have given two shits anyways.

This was a stepping stone for other opportunities in hospitality and a way to pay bills, nothing further, which led to a high staff turnover. Leigh had been there a year though which basically made her part of the furniture, but still not one that any of the male staff would be allowed to sit on.

She wanted more.

She wanted a man who would come into her life and sweep her away from the uncontrolled libidinousness of Cheam's Wetherspoons. 'The moon over the waves' was not aptly titled as there was neither anything luminous nor calm about the establishment. Leigh called it 'The Hell near the cesspit' which was closer by far to the truth.

Wistfully, she wiled the rest of her shift away, drowning out both staff and clientele, achieving the barest of minimum. The beachfront postcard comments of some of the older men went faux giggled, and lecherous eyes were avoided.

Leigh was in her last year in her twenties and was exceptional in the eyes of all the eager males. Her five-foot-seven height made her imposing as she was not slender, due to hours of cross-training sessions in the gym, she cut a figure of feminine force that attracted the overly ambitious.

She wanted more from life.

She wanted the excitement seen on wild Instagrams, and influencing TikToker feeds, even knowing it was ninety per cent faked.

Jo entered, interrupting her chain of thought.

"You're done Leigh hun, time to be free of this fucking shit hole," she replied monotonously, in full earshot of Derek, the regular alcoholic. He looked up trying to comprehend the words from his pickled synapses. He looked down again to his drink as Jo poured him another one, which was way over the limit. His wallet was on the counter, and she tapped it, paying for him.

"Cheers babes. Stay safe tonight. Oh, and Clive's on a bit of a letchy rampage." Leigh warned, knowing that Jo could handle her own. It was a warning, more for the older manager though as Jo was quick to anger. Leigh gathered her personal items from the staff room, still seeing the misspelt cup located on the desk where she'd abandoned it pre-shift. Chucking it in the bin she walked out, happy to be free.

The early evening air was cooler than normal, so she put in her earpods for a distracted walk home. It would take her a ten-minute stride so cranked up the volume.

"Police tape, don't cross the line. It looks like there's been a crime," came belting out by the songstresses of Neoni, one of Leigh's favourite musical choices.

It was then that she felt the eyes upon her.

"Body bag. Thought you could put me in a body bag," continued the song as she looked around.

Nothing.

Wait.

There was a hooded figure across the road, standing there, hands buried deep within trouser pockets. The person was in a darkened spot on the pavement, shadows clouding any visible features. She quickened her pace, and whilst not scared, admitted to herself to being a little creeped out.

Her stride increased in length creating distance between the two people which relaxed her somewhat. Ahead, a crossing blinked red for pedestrians to stop, so she took the chance to look back. The hooded figure was now on the same side as she was, walking steadily towards her. Still a distance away, Leigh looked both ways and crossed.

The cyclist screamed out of nowhere, narrowly missing her by a matter of inches.

"Watch where you're going, you sketchy bitch!" was screamed back at her as the bike sped away. Leigh responded by calling him a 'lycra arsebag' and again quickened her pace. Completely, not fussed by the actual near miss because she just wanted to be home.

Looking back once more, she saw the figure again standing still, watching. She planned to lose whoever it was with a tried and tested manoeuvre. Getting to the corner of her road, she rounded the corner and ran the last few steps to the block where she lived; a mass of lovely flats hidden away above a car showroom.

As she got to the door, she threw it open and flung herself inside, driven on by the adrenaline.

She was absolutely sure that the hooded figure had not seen where she went, and more so, would never guess the flat number anyway.

Getting to her front door, she opened it and immediately was shocked by the man standing in her kitchen.

## Chapter Thirty Eight

### Stick, meet butt

### Leigh and Jack

Leigh was still pumped full of adrenaline at the shock of seeing someone in her home that she hadn't brought in herself and it pushed her mind into fight or flight mode.

It chose to fight.

She snatched up a kitchen knife from the rack on the surface and screamed at the intruder as forcefully as she could muster.

"What the fuck are you doing in my house?" Angrily she pointed the knife at him, realising for the first time that he was only wearing a towel around his waist. From across the room, the man turned slowly, raising his hands to show that he was not a threat. The towel shifted slightly due to the raising of his arms, and Leigh could now see his toned physique. She looked appraisingly up and down his body and admittedly in another setting would have jumped him like a rampant rabbit with fresh batteries. Her books of choice were filled with 'enemies to lovers' tropes and she toyed with the idea of shagging the almost naked burglar, as it was a plot straight from one of her spicy romance novels. The two conflicting emotions were playing havoc within her mind, and she jabbed the knife at him once more.

"Who are you? You're not anyone Vik would've brought in, as she's only obsessed with her boss. You can't be him because she says he's got a stick jammed up his butt."

It was Jack's turn to be confused.

From out of Vikki's bedroom flew the half-clothed,

recently shocked awake Vikki who ran to Leigh's side, alongside the all too familiar thud of bare feet on the floor.

"He's with me!!" she screamed in as reassuring a tone as she could to defuse the situation, which had become a little weird for all concerned. Leigh looked even more bewildered as Jack's towel slipped, and he quickly grabbed at it but before he did, both women saw everything that Vikki was obsessed with.

"Oh. Errrrr hi. I'm Jack," he said, offering one hand to shake while the other hastily covered himself. The girls looked at each other and burst out laughing.

***

"As initial first meetings go, that one will stand out," Leigh flirted, clearly attempting to fill each sentence with as much innuendo as possible.

"I think you'll find nothing was indeed 'standing out' at that time," Jack responded. Leigh blinked back at him, having not expected such a retort. She burst out laughing, almost snorting her wine in an unladylike manner.

All three laughed as much as they could remember ever doing as they had reacquainted themselves on this new, better footing. They'd ordered in and the food and wine flowed, causing all three to become a little light-headed. The reasons behind 'stick up the butt' had been raised and Vikki explained that due to Jack's organised outlook compared to her wild abandon, she thought that she would never have a single chance with the man she'd grown fond of. Never mind then falling for, head and heels colliding as she went.

The more the night went on, the more was exposed. Vikki admitted that she'd always had a crush on Jack, and that she should've made a move ages ago. Jack also admitted the same, but he was too much a stickler for his own rules. It made him realise that the stick comment was actually fair, and agreed with the analogy but explained that he too had fallen for the aspects that Vikki thought would hold her back. He had needed some chaos in his life for a long time now and this golden-haired temptress had brought it in droves.

"Well, I don't know about you both, but I need a bed," and mock yawned at the pair of them, overly exaggerating the movement. Vikki stood, and Jack ran an appraising eye over her body as memories from their first tryst in the car flooded his mind. He was still enraptured with her beauty, which was only enhanced by their immense trust in each other.

He noticed that when saying goodnight to Leigh, she kissed her full on the mouth, for longer than the expected time. She smiled up at her and nodded, an apparent knowing glance.

"I'm a very, very lucky man," He proclaimed to Leigh as he began following Vikki into her bedroom. Under her breath, Leigh said,

"I think you're about to get luckier..."

\* \* \*

I got into bed and waited eagerly for Vikki to join me, but she had gone back to the door, I assumed to switch off the light. To my surprise she opened it, leaving it wide open and stripping off the lounge clothes she'd thrown on. As she got into bed, I noticed Leigh had appeared in the doorway.

"Do you want this?" Vikki said, awaiting an answer, and my mind went into immediate overdrive. Is she doing this for me? Is she doing this because she thinks I want this? I don't want to upset her, but then, I don't want to appear prudish. Fuck. I was overthinking. Say something, dumbass!

"Only if you do." It had as much conviction as I could muster. Vikki smiled as Leigh started removing her clothes.

## Chapter Thirty Nine

Fuck me...

## Chapter Forty

### Tuesdays are for threesomes

### Jack

I awoke sore. Like I'd run a marathon. Hard. Not in that way, but in the strenuous normal version. I couldn't move due to the soreness and the fact that I was pinned down on either side.

Very, very happily pinned, mind you.

I twiddled the fingers on my right hand and the movement brought a wave of pins and needles flashing through each digit. Leigh was lying on her side stretched out, with one leg drawn up. Her head using my bicep as a cuddle toy; with my arm fully extended under her.

Cradled in my right arm though was Vikki who, in her sleep had managed to hug my entire right side, snuggling into me as best she could. Craning, I looked at her and knew this was it. I felt her full body length and it felt right. It felt as whole as anyone could.

I hoped that she would be my all, and our lives would change forever, for the better. I know, it's only been actual days, but it just worked. I wasn't looking forward to the chat with the inspector though. I planned to move teams to offset the relationship and had run through the conversation I was going to have, adding in the benefit to both the borough and the incoming team. I always tried to make everything I did a benefit, rather than a hindrance as it was always hard to argue against your own best interest. This way every party in every negotiation would be satisfied. I thought about mentioning Leigh, but in that discussion, she was irrelevant, this just being a very happy addition. No offence meant obviously. Plus, I wasn't one to brag. My sex life was nobody's business, not even to bombast about the wildness of the last few days. It was disrespectful to Vikki, and by default, now Leigh, so I decided to shield both women's honour from any office gossip. Truthfully, it was only Vikki that was important to me. In all aspects.

Carefully, I managed to extricate my arm from underneath Leigh, and she grumbled and rolled flat, still lost in hopefully pleasant dreams. It took all my restraint to not smack her bum, but I watched as it settled into a peaceful rest. Glancing around, I took in the full state of the room. Clothes were everywhere, joined on the floor with bed covers and zero care for the normal cloth-based filing systems of the outside world. I noticed the side table where the protection I'd used on Leigh was wrapped securely for disposal as I'd left it last night. I should've disposed of it already, but after my performance in the athletics department last night, I was all but done. The girls had been dreamlike in their beauty for the hours we were together. I'd never done anything like this. While I was honoured to have the two of them together, it was also so different. I'd shagged Leigh but made love to Vikki at the same time. A weird experience to feel at the same moment. Vikki had again insisted on feeling my every inch within her and I reminded myself to have a talk about birth control when appropriate. But she felt SO good, and seeing her free was my drug of choice. I don't care about anything else in the world but her.

It was then that the phone rang, shocking both of us into work mode.

# Chapter Forty One

## Autopilot

## Jack

Even though our shift wasn't supposed to start until 14:00 hours, Vikki and I flew into action. Several local officers had been called up to manage a demonstration that was bringing the A3 dual carriageway to a standstill. This meant that backfilling was going to be the name of the game and people from all across the borough were volunteering. The call-up hadn't mentioned what the cause being fought was for, and I couldn't for the life of me think what relevance a main road to the coast could've done to offend anyone.

"My money is on Just Stop Oil." Said Vikki who was hurriedly trying to find something clean to wear in the mountain of clothes scattered all over the room. For one moment, I thought she didn't actually own a wardrobe as I'd not noticed one. (My attention was always diverted. Sue me). But she did, and it was open and had a trail of clothes spilling from it too. It had the look of vomiting a collection of strappy tops, undergarments, and other clothing as if it had overeaten a Primark the night before. As I dressed, I noticed that her bedroom was as chaotic as she was, and the strewn clothes seemed to be trying to make some sort of feminine material diorama as items were everywhere.

"People want to stop oil? By making cars, which use oil, go slower?" The logic was lost on me and Vikki thought on the sentence for a second, nodded in agreement, and carried on getting dressed.

I knew I should be giving her space to do so, and

concentrating on getting myself ready, but I couldn't help it. I stole a look at her. Seeing her made me smile. I made a few mental notes at this point.

⬥ I must tell the inspector - Gotta have this above board.

⬥ I love her.

⬥ I really needed to organise this room.

Wait. I scrolled the list back in my head. 'I love her.' Things weren't added to my mental fortress list if it wasn't true. It just is now. Maybe I should tell her? Now? No. Later. Fuck. (We'll do that later too). I finished dressing and ran to the kitchen where Leigh was already making coffee. I hadn't even noticed that she'd woken, got up, or even moved in our haste to get dressed. Such was my attention to Vikki, I mused. Leigh was great, don't get me wrong, but Vikki? Off the charts. The kettle pinged off as the steam rose and I noticed that she was making two coffees in to-go cups making me realise that she had ridden this police rollercoaster before. More often than was ever welcome, police officers of mostly the lower ranks would get called up when critical incidents happened, and life would be immediately dropped to help. It was great when you had someone supportive who knew the 'shit-hits-fan drill.' Coffee was a top priority as it was the lifeblood of the rushing officer. You always knew when you were in a copper's home as they normally had a cupboard filled with travel mugs, mostly scratched to hell.

My train of thought was derailed as Vikki entered the room. And then... kissed me. It was somehow unexpected and had no sexual undertones whatsoever. I cannot describe the feeling with the justice it deserved. She was there, and nothing else was. The room blended, melded into nothing and all that I could feel, and taste was her. It was an intense feeling better than anything I had ever felt before. It was beautiful. It was... It was just everything. As a grown man of epic levels of self-control, I lost all of it. My knees buckled and I steadied myself. It was my first kiss, and a final kiss all rolled into one beautiful moment. This was love. Love's very kiss, and the definition of what forever feels like. As I leaned into it, the world continued to fall away, leaving just the two of us suspended in this pulchritudinous moment.

My heart raced, a symphony of emotions pounding in my chest. Our lips met softly, lovingly, like the gentle touch of a feather. The warmth of her breath mingled with mine, and I felt a spark, a connection that went beyond the physical. I hadn't realised just how soft her lips were, and as they moved against mine, I could taste the sweetness of her affection. Each kiss was slow, deliberate, and filled with a tenderness that spoke of our shared history, of moments big and small that had brought us to this point. My hands cradled her face, as she wrapped hers behind me, and I felt the smoothness of her skin and the softness of her hair, and it anchored me in the reality of her presence. Time seemed to stretch, each second a lifetime of unspoken words and emotions which made me worry about being late to the recall to work, even though I knew these fleeting few seconds were not the lifetime that they felt.

I felt her smile against my lips, a small, beautiful curve that made my heart swell with love, so I pulled her closer, wanting to hold onto this feeling forever, to never let go of the warmth and the love that flowed between us. In that kiss, I poured all the love I had for her, hoping she could feel the depth of my feelings. It was a promise, a reassurance, and an expression of the profound connection we shared. As we slowly pulled away, our foreheads resting against each other, I opened my eyes to find her looking at me with the same love and adoration I felt.

It was at that moment, that briefest of seconds, that I felt my life begin. I knew that no matter what karma threw our way, we had this bond, this love that would carry us through. With a soft, contented sigh, I leaned in for one more kiss, already anticipating the countless moments of love we had yet to share. I closed my eyes and took a deep breath as she drew away, knowing full well, and feeling it herself, the power of the moment. I wanted to say "I love you," a thousand times right then and there. In the kitchen. Right now. But we had to go.

I promised myself I would tell her later.

# Chapter Forty Two

## Hold the castle

### Jack

The drive to the office was calm even if a tad hurried. A weird feeling given everything that had happened already that morning. We both felt what we could only describe as 'serene.' I made a note to look up the definition of happiness in the dictionary and send in an amendment if corrections were needed.

'happiness'

/hapns/

noun

The state of pleasurable contentment of mind; deep pleasure in or contentment with one's circumstances.

(Yeah. Fits well.)

I wanted to ask Vikki something as we drove, but my mind went into awkward teenager mode. So I blurted.

"Errrrr... So... Last night. Errrrr... Why, how?" Yup. Nailed it.

Vikki giggled at me, clearly knowing what I was stumbling over. She blushed and as I looked at her, the smile that I'd grown to really enjoy was there.

"I wanted you to have fun. Plus, me and Leigh are close. Always have been. She kinda hates when I have anyone back as she loves me all herself. Not that I had many back there, but you get what I mean!" It was her turn to blush and become the bumbling one.

"That's really fair. I'm glad." Was all I could muster. She smiled and giggled in the way she does.

Getting to the station, I dropped Vikki off around the corner. It wasn't that we were hiding our relationship because we were, but it was for a good reason. I wanted to tell the governor first, out of respect. He'd always had our backs which was fortunate as it really helped when you needed someone to go to bat for you. He realised, as I did, that if you look after your staff, you get more out of them, and more so, you're not being a dick to people. 'Treat others as you'd like to be treated,' and 'Never give a job to someone you wouldn't do yourself,' were the management mantras he had on his wall, although I wasn't sure if the quotes were correct. So, he deserved to hear directly from us first so we can best work this out for the job and us.

Even getting there at different times was a risk if it wasn't long enough as the gossip mill would churn no matter what, but I was trying. Going straight to the male locker room, I brushed off the dust of a uniform I hadn't worn in a while and was pleased to see that everything was still in order. It also still fits, which is every CID officer's nightmare. Being called up and finding that the job issue scratchy trousers also now cut off the circulation makes me shudder. I was fortunate enough that the white shirt was also steamed stiff so that the creases were all in the right place. Nice. There's no point going out if the first impression I give is that I look like I was impersonating an officer. Sliders and stripes were levelled perpendicular to the angle of the bottom and measured to the same distance from as each other. Perfection. I looked the part because it was a part I was born to play.

As I left the locker room which had a distinct smell of old Lynx Africa and workman's socks, I caught Vikki coming out of the ladies' changing room. A quick glance and I noticed that even through the anarchy that embodied her, she took the same pride in the uniform as I did.

I chanced a quick smile.

She smiled back.

Maybe I should tell her I love her now?

No. Later. Do it later.

\*\*\*

The CID office was abuzz with people running around getting their swans in order so that they could pull up the slack the demonstration was causing. Gareth was sitting in his usual seat, trying to eat a Dairylea Dunker with the smallest nacho crisp I'd ever seen. He had cheesy fingers because of it, and I saw that his keyboard was also sharing in his lunchtime snack. You could probably retype whatever he was writing as the keys were now more cheese-based than they ever should be.

Urgh.

I mentally noted to ensure that his area was fumigated and that all his stationery was burned in the backyard and replaced with new equipment upon his retirement. A few of the other teams were also in uniform having received the same task and I rallied them all to the briefing room. Some were not from my team, but they were the CID family, so I took the lead over all of them.

"James, hold the castle while we're gone," I said, handing over command to the younger detective constable.

"The fort sarge." He corrected me politely. I was never

one to get colloquialisms right, so I removed the castle from the saying, nodding back to James. I updated 'A man's home is his fort' as that must also be the correct venue vernacular.

Officers shuffled into seats; and awaited the briefing and postings for the shift.

With that, the briefing room decided our fate.

## Chapter Forty Three

### Always watching

### Watcher and the Wolf

That night, when they stood over the body of the young half-eaten girl, felt so long ago now and both Nathan and the wolf lusted to hunt again. It felt pivotal and was a moment that would change the lives of both the Watcher and White, the great wolf. As they stood amidst the crimson-stained earth, both their senses were ablaze with the intoxicating scent of the human flesh. White wanted more, and no longer wanted to hunt in the shadows. It was a hunger unlike any it had known before and it pulsed through White's veins, becoming a ravenous craving that clawed at its insides with a merciless ferocity. White's teeth gleamed like polished daggers, once again thirsting for the taste of warm blood upon its tongue. With each beat of the wolf's large heart, the desire to hunt, to consume, burned ever brighter, a fiery inferno consuming its very soul.

No longer content with the hunt for mere sustenance, White had discovered a voracious appetite for the essence of humanity itself, a hunger that could only be sated by the crimson rivers that flowed beneath the skin of its prey. As the beast prowled through the darkness of the room, it even considered eating its other, the Watcher, the host, but White knew the consequences of doing that all too well. It was an inbuilt memory that the host must not be eaten, as doing so would damn the wolf itself to death. White's eyes glowed with feral hunger, and it knew that it had become a creature of red, a predator whose thirst for blood knew no bounds. Unseen words passed between the two beings and the

Watcher knew the hunt was needed.

"It's too soon. We risk exposure," said Nathan to White, pleading while also secretly wanting it himself just as much. White gruffed annoyedly at his host and took a step forward, not aggressively, but to hone its point. It was needed. The recent kill had changed everything. No longer will they hunt in darkness. Now they were apex predators.

"No! Bad wolf!" Nathan chided, bopping the beast on its nose, trying not to show a glimmer of the fear that was rising within him.

Without warning, the massive jaws clenched around the hand, severing Nathan's little finger. The host yelped in pain as did the wolf, who retreated from the human, suddenly unable to bear weight on its lead paw. It sat down and licked at its appendage to see the smallest, the dewclaw, shrivel and turn into an inky fluid. It dripped to the floor leaving a glistening pool which, when the light caught it, shone with otherworldly greens and purples. The screaming in the background reminded White that this was of its own doing, and it had learned the consequences of its actions the hard way.

"If we were one, I'd still have a working hand you cunt dog! I birthed you!" screamed Nathan, as the initial fear dwindled away to anger born of the pain.

* * *

The host screamed and shouted for a while afterwards as it bandaged its hand. It had allowed the great wolf to eat the finger, hoping that it would satiate its growing hunger. It was tossed into the wolf's waiting maw with revulsion, but it did little to stop the gnawing in its stomach. The Watcher vomited into the corner of the room at the eagerness of the feast, but The wolf knew soon after that the delicate morsel was not even close.

As the host was distracted and his flurry of screamed obscenities over, White left the house unseen, creeping through a window and down into an alley, stealth only a passing thought on its hungry mind.

## Chapter Forty Four

### Dead ends

### Krystal

'Cashing up was such a drag,' thought Krystal as the shutters of the pink-fronted lingerie store clanked slowly down. She'd worked there for five years, and loved the freedom of expression it gave her, alongside the pay-cheque. She adored being able to assist couples with their lovemaking and joined in whenever the opportunity arose. She knew that it was taking customer servicing to a new level, but Krystal felt it was part of the overall service that she should offer. She especially loved that 'new lesbian smell' and could spot a closet leaver a mile off.

Krystal had always felt that she was a wild one at heart and counting the numbers on the receipt slips was a real dampener. All she wanted to do was flirt about getting customers inside and then get home in front of her camera to push her TikToks out to her loving audience. She'd mastered the dances, the air fryer recipes, and the 'follow if you're under 1k,' trends and was now trying makeup tutorials in fluffy pink bras. It was her niche, and she loved it, as did her ten thousand followers. Her comments section always blew up when she live-streamed, but she couldn't do a thing whilst here. Even the sneaky ones she took outside the shop had been banned by the manager, as it was 'her hobby, not her day job!'

As twenty-five-year-old Krystal stood behind her desk at work, her mind buzzed with a flurry of notifications from tonight's TikToks. Each ping felt like a tug, pulling her away from the mundane tasks in front of her and her fingers itched to grab her phone and film another quick video, to capture a moment, a joke, a dance move that could potentially skyrocket her follower count.

Instead, she found herself confined by the walls of the shop, her creativity stifled by counting the day's takings. With every passing minute, she felt the weight of missed opportunities, imagining the trending challenges and viral trends she could be participating in if only she were free.

As her co-workers would chat about their weekend plans and upcoming projects, Krystal's mind drifted to her very own happy world of TikTok fame. Often, she'd even start singing 'This ain't Texas…' mid conversation such was her online addiction. She longed to be out in the open, filming under the sun or editing in her cosy bedroom flat, where she felt most alive and in her element. The tick of the clock on the wall seemed to mock her, each second stealing away her precious time to create and connect with her audience. She couldn't help but feel a sense of frustration, trapped between the demands of her job and the allure of social media stardom.

Yet, despite her longing to break free, Krystal knew she had to bide her time. She couldn't afford to jeopardise her job, not when it provided the stability she needed to pursue her passions. So, with a heavy heart and a determined spirit, she buried her impatience and focused on the task at hand, flicking the coins into the money bag.

'Looked about right' she thought, closing the till and stuffing all the receipts into a safe bag. It was time. Her counting down of the minutes until she could escape the confines of the shop had finally ticked to zero and she knew that soon she'd be diving back into the world of TikTok, where she truly belonged.

Slamming the back door, she checked that it was locked, then checked again. She remembered the safety talk the local police had given to shops in an effort to prevent late-night burglaries. The thought of the police brought back the memory of the passing of her local officer. She missed PC Alex. He was always smiling and nice to all the businesses and residents.

"Sad times," she said out loud.

Shrugging, she pushed the memory back down, covered by Benson Boone's viral track 'Beautiful Things' which she thought to use in tonight's reel. 'Slowed down, sped up or remixed though?' She would have to consider the content to see what worked best.

The pink fluffy scarf she chose to wear contrasted with the moon's eerie glow, and Krystal waited for the bus to take her most of the way home. Living in Surrey had its perks, but public transport was not one of them. Wishing she'd learned to drive she remembered that she'd given it up due to not being allowed to learn in six-inch platforms. People got on and off and some even noticed the pink fluffy dressed woman, but Krystal's thoughts were lost online throughout the journey. She dinged out a tune on the bus's bell and waited for the vehicle to stop, which it dutifully did, leaving her to walk the rest of the way home. She was singing to the song blaring into her air pods, oblivious to the world around her.

***

The hulking beast in the alley loomed in the shadows, its predatory gaze fixed on Krystal as she teetered down the dimly lit path in her absurdly fluffy pink attire and sky-high heels. Unaware of the danger stalking her, Krystal hummed the tune, lost in a world all her own, while her mind was preoccupied with thoughts of her upcoming trend chasing.

White watched on, its snout twitching with anticipation, and crept closer, its claws scraping against the pavement. With each step, the sheer absurdity of the situation heightened, as Krystal's flamboyant outfit clashed hilariously against the imminent threat lurking behind her.

The wolf licked its lips. He was going to enjoy every bite.

## Chapter Forty Five

### No dogs allowed

### Vikki

Officers were divided into the remaining response team members and a covering officer so they weren't thrown into the wild without some sort of support. Vikki was placed in the response car for the fast-time calls, her assuming the position of operator, for the well-experienced driver. She wasn't worried as she had been in this role many times in her career as her quick thinking complimented it well.

Vikki noted that Jack had been offered a desk role to hand out the jobs and monitor from a supervisory role, but he'd opted to go out on foot patrol with one of the team. She smiled that he'd chosen to be proactive and work with response, but secretly she wished they could be partnered up together. Smiling, she watched as he donned the lurid fluorescent yellow of the high-visibility jacket and strode out into the early afternoon.

Calls began flowing in, with them being snatched up by the various teams available, keeping the area car free for the more fast-paced calls. This was a solid tactic as this BMW was the fleet's finest and fastest. The computer filled up with calls, units became assigned and the shift just kept carrying on. Hours passed and people were helped as best officers could, but they were clocking up.

⬥ A domestic report involving a drunk female...

⬥ Shoplifting in progress - unit on scene - one male in cuffs... Van unit required.

⚔ Theft of pedal cycle - area search - no trace currently...

⚔ It was quickly becoming a standard shift.

Vikki was getting to know her new colleague, PC James Carter. He was a dedicated and seasoned police officer with a career spanning over 15 years, and he spent his entire tenure in the fast response unit, a role he was both passionate about and highly skilled in. Known among his colleagues as 'Speedy Carter,' he had a reputation for his quick reflexes, sharp instincts, and an uncanny ability to remain calm under pressure. Vikki liked him more and more as the shift went on.

Speedy operated the high-performance vehicle equipped with the latest technology to handle emergencies swiftly and efficiently. His car was outfitted with advanced communication systems, GPS, and a state-of-the-art inter-aural phase difference siren and lighting system to navigate through traffic quickly and safely. While sitting, she could not do it to him for justice, but from the yard to the car, she noticed him standing at a full six feet tall with a sturdy build. He exuded confidence and authority, and his short-cropped hair and clean-shaven face presented a professional and approachable demeanour.

If she wasn't taken already, she would've been as his piercing blue eyes were oceanic droplets anyone could swim in. But she was taken. She smiled at the thought, feeling blood rushing to areas that reminded her of Jack. The radio clattered to life though and ruined Vikki's brief aside.

"SR200 receiving?" Vikki noted the vehicle's call sign and responded. "Area car receiving, Surrey Control..." She said, awaiting a reply.

"Thank you. All units are assigned, can you take a non-griefy call? Apparently, a male is shouting his head off about a dog bite and causing a breach of the peace. Might be just words of advice, but can you take it?" Vikki confirmed that they would, and the details of the shout were taken by the pair without objection. They headed towards the venue, keeping in mind that if anything else came in that was more urgent, they would ditch this for that. Vikki went through the details, reporting everything of note to her driver.

"Should be an intel report to the Safer Neighbourhoods Teams at worst, but we'll check it out. The male mentioned is not known to us and shows no warning markers. Apparently, the informant is pissed as the flats are not allowed any animals," Vikki informed, acknowledging that she would cover the paperwork for Speedy.

As night began to fall, their ETA clicked down to four minutes.

# Chapter Forty Six

## Then there was only darkness

### Krystal

The night was getting dark, with a moon in its waxing gibbous stage, just a day or two before it shone its fullest. The eerie moonlit glow melded with the lights of Epsom High Street as Krystal walked the last section of her journey home. She felt a shiver run down her spine as she walked through the cool night air, pulling what little clothes she wore tighter around her.

The streets were deserted, as all the shops had ceased their day's trade, and the silence was always unsettling. Krystal loved the noise and the attention her presence garnered, showing her to be something different, even wild. But tonight, she walked briskly, her footsteps echoing in the empty streets and alleyways. She had always been a bit jumpy after dark when no one was around, but tonight something felt different, more menacing even. She quickened her pace, her senses on high alert.

A noise disturbed her thoughts. A rustling sound, like something moving through the nearby bushes. She stopped and turned, scanning the shadows. Nothing. Krystal shook her head, trying to shake off the feeling of being watched, and continued walking. She wished she were further into town but living on the outskirts, there was a marked difference in footfall where she was.

And the sense of unease grew stronger.

As she rounded the corner onto a narrow, dimly lit street, she saw it. At first, it was just a pair of glowing silver eyes in the darkness, then the shape emerged—a large, white wolf, its fur almost luminescent in the early moonlight. Krystal's heart pounded in her chest as she froze, her breath catching in her throat. The wolf growled a deep, guttural sound that sent a wave of terror through her. It seemed to be meant for her to hear, a threat that was created to frighten. She took a step back, then another, before turning and running as fast as she could. She could hear the beast behind her, its powerful limbs propelling it forward with terrifying speed. Krystal darted down an alley, hoping to lose the creature in the maze of backstreets. Her legs burned, and her breath came in ragged gasps, but she didn't dare slow down. She could hear the wolf's heavy breathing and the sound of its claws scraping against the pavement.

Bolting around a corner she stopped sharply.

Dead end.

The tall brick wall blocked her path, and panic surged right through her as she looked around frantically for an escape route, but there was nowhere to go. As she turned, the wolf's shadow loomed larger as it approached, seemingly filling all available space.

Its eyes were fixed on her, its teeth bared.

Desperate, Krystal pressed her back against the wall, her mind racing. She tried to scream, but no sound came out. The wolf stopped a few feet away, its eyes gleaming with a predatory hunger. It bared its teeth, a low growl rumbling from its chest.

"Please, no," was all Krystal could manage and it came out as a whisper, as the tears streamed down her face. She felt a surge of hopelessness and the crushing weight of knowing that her death could be imminent as the wolf moved steadily closer.

Krystal's legs crumpled beneath her.

She sat, her arm outstretched, trying to silently plead for mercy from the beast in front of her. She was frozen, incapable of movement, as if the slightest flinch would cause the beast to launch itself forward. But the closer it came. Inching, slowly forward. The closer it came until she could smell the fur, the breath, the entire presence. The white wolf moved closer still and as it got to her outstretched arm, it opened its mouth. Slowly, Krystal watched, stunned into paralysis as her arm disappeared into the beast's mouth. She could feel the heat, the moisture in the gaping maw, and saw her arm disappear to almost the elbow before the jaws clamped shut. Pain tore through her, somehow from the area where her arm should have been. The phantom pain clouded her judgement to insanity as she waved her remaining hand through the space where her bitten off arm should have been. Her arm was severed, and the pain racked up the remaining limb, to a mind now broken by the terror of what was happening. Blood spurted from the wound and splattered over the wolf's face which she noticed was chewing. It gulped down the morsel slowly as if showing the power it had over her.

The last thing Krystal saw was the wolf's snarling, blood-covered face, its eyes locked onto hers. Then there was only darkness.

## Chapter Forty Seven

### Someone's hiding something...

### Vikki

"Knock again?" Vikki said to Speedy as they waited at the reported address. They'd spoken to the initial caller who explained that the man upstairs was the 'weird one you get in every block' and she was always hearing clattering of some sort. She went on about how she'd complained to the housing association many, many times, but nothing was ever done. Speedy had dutifully listened attentively to how it was different in her day and that she blamed Brexit for lazy landlords. When the elderly tenant started on about her hip operation, he tactfully got the subject back on to her call and bade her farewell.

The door upstairs was as decrepit as the block was, but sturdy enough to bear the brunt of the police constable's hearty knock. Going upstairs, Vikki realised what the woman was on about. 'It looked simply... rough. Not crime rough, but not somewhere you'd want to visit,' thought Vikki, vowing to wash her entire uniform when she got home.

Speedy knocked again.

"Fuck off!" came the welcoming reply.

"Sir, it's the police. Can we please have a quick word? One of your neighbours is worried about you." Vikki chimed in, ignoring the homeowner's first outburst. Vikki always allowed one emotional eruption before raising her vocal level, as you never knew what a person was going through. Tempers could flare for tragic reasons, so she would always give a second chance.

"Tell that old cunt to fuck off." And with that, both officers decided that he'd lost his second chance.

"Sir. Open the door please." Speedy lowered his tone to be both authoritative and non-threatening. 'Well, maybe just a little threatening,' thought Vikki smiling as the locks started unbolting from the other side. Multiple bolts, grips and latches clattered and unclasped, and the officers looked at each other, trying to count how many there were. The door opened and a man filled the gap, as the smell of a dog filled their nostrils. They both took a step back, reeling from the assaulting smell.

He explained that his name was Nathan and as Speedy went through the relevant details of the call, a police description filled Vikki's head, and she mentally checked through the details of the man in front of them.

⋏ Male, IC1 (which means 'white' to the uninitiated), slim but muscular build, possibly mid-fifties, long greying hair, wearing a t-shirt, faded jogging bottoms and one sock. Smelt of dog. Heavily.

When she moved to the description of his mentality, and general behaviour, she reeled for another reason.

Nathan's very presence sent a chill down her spine and a sight that elicited both pity and fear. His clothes, a mismatched ensemble of outdated garments, were covered in white pet hair, as if they had not been washed, along with the rest of the abode, in a very long time. Nathan's hair was long and greasy, falling in tangled strands around his gaunt, pale face, ending in a patchy equally unkempt beard. It framed a mouth that rarely formed anything other than a sinister smirk. His eyes were perhaps the most unsettling aspect, as they oozed a cold, calculating, darkness while they darted around furtively as constantly on the lookout for something.

Or someone.

Vikki immediately got the feeling that he was hiding something devastating and thought to motion themselves inside his flat for a further search but couldn't think of grounds worthy enough to justify it legally. She was sure the glint of malice in his eyes was a darkness that suggested he harboured ill intentions. Even Speedy seemed to find the conversation unsettling. Nathan's voice was low and gravelly, each word dripping with an unnerving calm that belied a possible threat lurking beneath his seemingly benign exterior. Disquietingly aloof screamed serial killer in all the television shows she watched, and Nathan fit all the stereotypes. What Vikki could see past him was a decrepit, dimly lit flat that seemed frozen in time, as the wallpaper peeled and even the musty air was trying to escape. It carried the faint scent of something stale and decaying. Despite his unkempt appearance, there was something unnervingly meticulous about Nathan. Everything in his flat, though chaotic at first glance, seemed to have a specific place, as if this man in front of Vikki followed a hidden, sinister logic. As Speedy continued to explain why they were there, Nathan was muttering to himself, as if they weren't really two police officers in full uniform standing right in front of him. As his eyes darted down the hallway, Vikki's attention was brought to the fact that he was actively hiding his arm behind him. She nodded the information to Speedy, who picked it up, changing the conversation's course.

"Sir, is everything OK? Do you have something behind your back?" Speedy wanted to know. He took a slight step back and angled himself ready to deal with whatever the man might produce. Vikki noticed the blood droplet on the floor as Nathan grew anxious in front of them.

"What? No! Leave me alone!" Stepping back, he motioned to close the door, but Speedy lived up to his namesake, putting his boot in the door crack.

"Have you hurt yourself, sir?" Vikki asked calmly to show that she wanted to offer any help he needed.

"No! It's just a cut! I don't want your help!" He pushed against the door, using both hands to try and wedge the larger officer out of his home. It didn't take an investigative mind to see that Nathan's hand was wrapped in a bloodstained sock. Vikki immediately called for the London Ambulance to attend as the blood loss seemed more than just a cut, as it was colouring the material in differing shades of scarlet. Although she was unaware of the extent of the damage, she surmised that it had been bleeding for a lengthy time.

"LEAVE!" Nathan shouted. "I don't want anybody else!"

With that, the door slammed shut.

And the radio burst into life.

# Chapter Forty Eight

## No way out

### Vikki

"Any available units, report to Epsom High Street for an area search. Details have been sent to your CAD terminals, but we have declared a critical incident. One female body has been found deceased. An unknown number of outstanding suspects."

Speedy and Vikki looked briefly at each other and raced down the steps in unison, taking most flights two at a time. Whilst they both wanted creepy Nathan to get help, they had to prioritise, and the ambulance was en route to help him. They wished they could see it through, but they both got the feeling this was a big thing. Critical incidents were not declared lightly as they put the wind up a lot of the top brass and local council partners.

Getting to the car, Vikki pulled up the details about a mutilated body found in an alleyway. There was a witness who had chanced upon it as they were taking the bins out, only to be scarred for their life. They had reported seeing a large white dog the size of a small horse, which was being investigated for its voracity.

"I hope it's not too bad a scene. Normal people are not made to deal with the sights we see," said Speedy, clearly worried for both the victim and the witness. Almost immediately, both officer's minds went through the bodies they'd seen.

⅄ The one being worked on, while blood pooled against an open eye.

⅄ The elderly woman who died in her sleep, rigored

into rigidity.

⚴ The sister hanging from a tree.

Vikki ripped the last one from her mind, fighting back the rising panic. Whilst she had not physically seen her sister deceased, officers had. They had to deal with everything that meant. The pair of officers were on scene in mere minutes, and out of the car as the tent was being erected around the body. Vikki caught sight of what was left of the poor victim, as an officer to her left vomited into a dustbin. Officers all around her looked shocked and broken as they milled about, trying to comprehend what they had seen.

Vikki watched as a pink-furred boot, heavily blood-splashed, was photographed. What hit her most was that some of the victim's leg was still protruding from it. Again, the officer vomited violently into the bin, and Vikki noticed that Jack was standing next to him, with his hand on his back in clear support. The skipper looked over at Vikki and a silent conversation happened between the pair.

Jack - [Are you OK? It's a bad one. Be careful.]

Vikki - [Fine, I will. Wolf?]

Jack - [Wait for confirmation]

Care was exchanged between them without any need for words. Vikki and Speedy were assigned to patrol around the immediate area and Jack was given foot patrol along the high street. His officer was allowed back to the office for a comfort break and more importantly, a toothbrush. Words of caution were given to all gathered officers by the inspector and they dispersed, trying to both reassure the public and find any evidence of what the hell had happened.

It had been mere minutes from the initial call, but all gathered knew that this was as critical as it could get. There was a wolf loose.

# Chapter Forty Nine

## Darkness rises

### Jack and Vikki

Seven minutes later, chaos won.

Eight minutes later, lives changed.

Vikki was on foot patrol as Speedy slowly shadowed her in the car. Whilst both officers wanted the safety of the vehicle, Speedy was assigned as driver so he drove, much to his annoyance. Vikki was walking where the car couldn't, checking down the alleyways and delivery areas hidden from view.

Neither knew who, or what they'd find, as the victim, the mutilated body, had been ravaged by God knows what. Reportedly a wolf, but how could it? The Chief Inspector designated as Gold in charge of the scene had called in literally everyone. Dog units were flying to the location as were the support units armed with heavy-duty equipment a beat officer could only dream of.

Whoever it was would be covered in blood.

The savageness of the attack would've meant arteries painting the attacker. It was clear that the suspect was up close and personal with the victim, blood would be everywhere.

Rounding a dark corner, Vikki came eye to eye with the massive, blood-covered, white wolf.

\*\*\*

This is straight out of a nightmare.

I knew that Vikki would be alright as she was in the

area car and that was at least something. Also, my young response police chaperone was going to be at the base being looked after, so he, whilst green and traumatised, would also be ok.

That was two people out of this nightmare which was a small mercy. All I'd ever wanted was that people were safe from harm and this was anything but. I'd arrived on scene before Vikki and got the tent arranged as a matter of urgency, as the thought of this hitting the news cycle filled me with dread. Also, I didn't want the general public seeing the scene either as even I was feeling the sight burned into my brain. You never get used to it. This mess or gore had been a person. Even in that condition, still someone's family. My thoughts were a turmoil of lists, and I was ticking through them to make sure I covered every base and crossed every T.

Vikki. On foot.

She was ahead of me, at an alleyway junction. I saw her disappear around a corner and felt my heart fall.

\*\*\*

Vikki looked into the deep silver eyes of the large snow-covered wolf with a crushing fear, yet also tinged with wonder at the how and why of the situation. This wolf was big. Too big. It shouldn't exist. But it did.

She could smell death on it. See the blood and viscera covering the snowy white fur. See its tongue lick hungrily at its lips.

Cautiously, she took tentative steps backwards as the beast rose to its full height.

One step. Two.

She was at the cross of the alley junction and considered running, but calculated correctly that the wolf was faster.

Three steps. Four.

The wolf leapt.

\*\*\*

I saw Vikki retreat from the junction and ran towards her. There was something she was seeing, out of my sight line that had scared her. Something she wanted to be further away from. Something I was going to put myself in the way of.

I reached the junction at full steam as a large white blur of fur erupted from the darkness towards Vikki.

\*\*\*

She knew there was nothing she could do now. In the second it took the beast to launch itself at her, she'd gone through every angle, each option a loss. Run? Dodge? Fight? Flee? Beg? All ended in her death. Silently, she prayed that it wouldn't hurt, that she'd die before pain had time to register. As her eyes began to close for what she thought was the last time, Jack flew at the beast, catching it mid-flight, and knocking it safely away.

\*\*\*

Momentum and fear for Vikki drove my actions as the briefest of thought for myself evaporated. This thing was huge, and it wasn't going to do what it did to that poor girl to my Vikki. Even, if it meant my end. Even, if I would become a statistic in this wolf's rampage.

The speed of my run and the lucky timing meant that I was rolling with the beast away from Vikki as searing pain ripped through my body. I knew it had bitten me almost immediately as sharp pincers of pain ripped through my shoulder. It caused me to loosen my hold enough for the beast to get free and it finished its interrupted flight in the street. It rolled and tumbled until the kinetic energy allowed it to steady itself on its side. Shrugging the impact off, it stood, reaching its full height. Now illuminated, I could see its actual size. It looked straight out of a nightmare as it was covered in blood, its white fur stained with death.

I needed to be ready for the impending retaliatory attack, so I got to my feet to brace for it. I knew I was still in between it and Vikki, so took strength from that small mercy. Glancing down, I saw that my high visibility jacket which once was yellow, was now heavily blood-stained. I wasn't sure how much of it was mine or cast off from the beast's violent attack earlier in the night. It was almost irrelevant at that point.

"Jack!" It was Vikki. Behind me. Safe. Deal with her safety after the massive wolf in front of me was out of the picture.

I chanced a glance back at her, trying to impel her to run, but she was an officer, so she was already moving to help me, despite both our peril. I needed to make more space between myself and Vikki, to give her more of a chance at life, one I wished I could be in after tonight.

I turned back to see the wolf lean backwards into an attack posture, ready to propel it forward towards me. In a second it would be on me, and I would not have the same element of surprise I had earlier. This copper's luck was evaporating fast.

As the beast leapt, it did not see the speeding police car off to its left. It hit the wolf square on its flank, ramming it away and out of my sight, with an audible yelp of pain and shock.

It was at that point that the blood loss took hold and darkness enveloped my senses.

## Chapter Fifty

### Lives reborn

### 1983

As Nathan wandered through the dense forest, the cool night air sent shivers down his spine. The moon hung forebodingly low in the sky, casting an ethereal glow upon the landscape. He felt a strange sense of peace wash over him, even with the renting pain in his chest and ear. If not for the searing pain arcing through his body, he imagined that he could have been lost in the dream state of the woods. The wounds were beginning to become strangely numb though, and sticky to the touch. The blood had stopped seeping from the various wounds and rents in his body now, and Nathan was thankful for such a small mercy.

Where was he?

After the beast attacked, he thought he was wandering home through an unconscious need for safety and security. He'd found himself in the middle of nowhere and the feeling of stillness in the night became a welcome respite from the chaos of his thoughts. He became blissfully unaware of all pain, both mental and physical as he drifted further into the woods. He felt like he was losing himself to bliss but just as he began to relax into the quietude of the forest, Nathan's senses heard a low growl emanating from the shadows ahead. His heart quickened with fear as he peered into the darkness, trying to discern the source of the sound.

His heart sank as he realised that it was the grey creature from earlier. Fear streaked through him, and he thought to run, but, like a ghost emerging from the mist, the grey wolf stepped into view. Its eyes gleamed with an otherworldly light, and Nathan felt a chill run down his spine at the sight of its feral beauty. For a moment, man and beast stood locked in a silent standoff, each sizing the other up with wary curiosity. Then, without warning, the wolf laid itself down in front of him, as if waiting for something to happen.

The pain that had seared through Nathan's body earlier had evaporated completely now. He was left with a dull numbness as he became lightheaded and disoriented, his senses swimming as he tried to make sense of what had and was happening.

Trance-like, Nathan felt a strange energy coursing through his body. It was as if every cell in his being was alight with newfound vitality, filling him with a sense of strength and power he had never known. Along with the surge of energy came a profound sense of change. Nathan could feel something stirring deep within him, a primal force awakening from its slumber. It felt like something was clawing through his system, moving and undulating through his internal organs. He felt them move and push around within his chest cavity but somehow, he felt no pain.

In a daze, Nathan hit the floor, virtually unconscious and barely feeling the woodland undergrowth underneath him. He lay there as the tearing sound began. It was coming from behind him, a ripping of meat, tearing, splitting.

He felt nothing.

Trying to crane his head backwards in the blur that used to be his senses, he watched as his spine rose from the remnants of his torso, the mass forming into something he was unable to comprehend. He thought the hallucination was due to loss of blood, that this nightmare was somehow a fevered dream his muddled senses were putting together.

He watched as the white wolf cub fell sideways, out of the gaping rent in his back that he could not fully see. It had though, quite clearly, been born from out of his body. It landed, bloody and small, on Nathan's right side.

He had a semblance that the gaping wound that was his back was reknitting itself together, except for this mass that he'd expelled, or birthed. He laughed in his mind as the situation broke down all remaining barriers to sanity. In seconds, he'd been torn asunder, but now, he was healing rapidly, as skin, bone, muscle and tissues knitted themselves back together. New organic material had grown to fill the void, remaking him anew.

The sight and feel of something truly otherworldly had shattered the fragile construct of his weakened mind, leaving behind a fractured remnant of sane comprehension. The once-steadfast pillars of sanity had crumbled beneath the weight of the inexplicable, as reality seemed to unravel before Nathan's eyes. At that moment, his mind had become a battleground between the familiar realms of rationality and the incomprehensible abyss of the unknown.

The unknown had won out.

His eyes were wide with terror and his mouth in a silent scream. Nathan grappled with a truth so alien. This was so utterly beyond the scope of his understanding, that it rendered his psyche asunder. Every fibre of his being strained against the unfathomable, struggling to reconcile the mundane with the cosmic.

In the end, he was left adrift in a sea of madness, forever haunted by the harrowing glimpse into the abyss. Something, no one should have to bear witness to.

As Nathan passed out, he saw the grey wolf meticulously clean the wolf cub of the blood of its birth until all that was left was the snowy white of its fur. It then picked it up gently and placed it next to Nathan, who was now its host, its watcher. The cub curled next to him, craving warmth and security.

The grey wolf backed away, disappearing into the darkness as swiftly as it had appeared.

\*\*\*

In the days that followed, Nathan found himself grappling with his newfound identity. He was the host, the watcher. The bite of the wolf had changed him in ways he could scarcely comprehend, blurring the lines between man and beast. Nathan and White were part of one whole, but separate being. But far from feeling afraid, Nathan felt a sense of liberation, unlike anything he had ever experienced. No longer shackled by the confines of his human existence, he roamed with White with a newfound sense of purpose, revelling in the raw beauty of the natural world. They knew that if they were ever found by the humans, they'd be torn apart, literally and figuratively. Their very existence brought a myriad of questions they could not answer.

Although he still bore the scars of his lonely past, Nathan no longer felt alone. For in the company of the wolf that now called him brother, he had found a sense of belonging that he had long thought lost.

Each day brought along new challenges and

adventures, as Nathan embraced his split nature with a fierce determination. He knew that his path would not be easy as he now faced the future with a courage born of the wild. He knew that he was no longer bound by the limitations of his past. He scoured the internet for the answers and when none came, he dug ever deeper into the darkest corners of the web. Each strand bore him new information of a world under his own and he loved every new pathway he found.

He was part of the hunt, the apex of the food chain.

As the moon rose high in the night sky each night, casting its silver light upon the world below, Nathan would throw back his head and let out a howl that echoed through the forests. A loud otherworldly defiant cry of triumph and rebirth.

He knew that he was finally free.

# Chapter Fifty One

## Thursday's are for comas

### Jack

When I first came out of the coma, it felt like emerging from the depths of a thick, impenetrable fog. Within that gloom, I thought it was a good idea to take a swim in a large bowl of custard. Whilst wearing pyjamas. To collect a brick or something from the bottom.

Everything was disjointed and hazy. My senses were dulled and sluggish. I really struggled to make sense of the world around me. I'd been rushed straight to the hospital, my body barely had time to touch the alley's ground. The London Ambulance Service had done us proud as always, even though I had no recollection of anything they did. The first thing I became aware of though, was the sound. It was initially distant, muffled, like I was underwater, and it grew slowly clearer. It morphed into the rhythmic beeping of medical machines, the soft murmur of voices, and the occasional clatter of equipment. It took a moment before I could differentiate between them, each sound piercing through the haze and anchoring me back to reality. Opening my eyes was the next challenge. My eyelids felt like they weighed a tonne, and when I finally managed to lift them, the harsh, sterile light of the hospital room made me squint and blink rapidly. Everything was a blur, a wash of white and muted colours. Shapes moved around me, but they were indistinct, phantoms in my periphery. There was a strange sensation in my body, a mix of heaviness and detachment. My limbs felt foreign as if they didn't belong to me. I tried to move, but my muscles responded sluggishly, weak from disuse. Pain flickered at the edges of my awareness, a dull, constant throb that seemed to emanate from everywhere and nowhere at once. Breathing was laborious, every breath, a conscious effort. I could feel the tube in my throat, an invasive presence that made swallowing difficult and speaking impossible. Panic flared briefly, but it was quickly smothered by a wave of exhaustion. Time was becoming an enigma, long forgotten. Seconds stretched into what felt like hours, and moments of clarity were interspersed with bouts of confusion and disorientation. Memories surfaced sporadically, fragments of the life I once lived, nightmares roaring up from my past. They were intermingled with strange, vivid dreams that left me questioning what was real.

Faces began to come into focus, leaning over me with expressions of concern and relief. I recognized some of them. Colleagues were standing alongside the doctors, but their features were distorted, as if I was seeing them through a frosted glass. Their voices, though clearer now, seemed to come from a great distance, echoing in my mind.

Vikki. Where was Vikki?

I tried to move but realised that my strength was not there. Plus, I began feeling someone else was on the bed alongside me. As the tube was removed, I felt Vikki raise herself up and hug me, tears streaming down her face. Immediately she was covering me with kisses, which felt strangely electric in my hazed state.

"Well, the cats out of the bag then Vikki." was all I could muster.

## Chapter Fifty Two

### Unknown days

### Jack

It felt like I'd lost track of days after waking up in the hospital, but apparently, it had only been two of them. I was in and out of a groggy state, not knowing what the hell was going on. The one thing, I was sure of, was that Vikki did not leave my side. I remember conversations with the inspector, and that we had sorted out an interim arrangement for our romantic situation. Not with the inspector, but with Vikki and me. I don't know why that needed clarifying. I blame the comma. He was good about it and understanding. Especially, after I apologised for not telling him before I was attacked by the giant white wolf.

"Jack, we'll monitor it and have a chat after our current critical is dealt with." He said, telling me that I'd probably saved Vikki's life.

"Vikki's Body Worn Video has made you a hero to the ranks, Jack." He'd added, smiling with pride.

"Tell that to my shoulder," was all I could reply. It had been fully bandaged and redressed daily as it healed, but the ache of the attack was a constant reminder of that night. The doctors were happy to discharge me after they saw it healing and the number of shots they'd pumped into me would stop any infection I might have picked up.

Gareth had even ventured out of the office too, brought to see me by Jim.

"Bitten by a wolf? Awwwwwwwooooooooo!" was what

he brought to the party. Everyone thought it was funny, but I didn't.

I had to tell Vikki something.

Something long forgotten.

Something I'd buried.

\*\*\*

Getting home, I realised Cat had been fed daily by a mix of Leigh and my sister. Vikki's flatmate and Cat, both animals in different ways, had grown quite fond of each other which was nice, but Leigh had very clearly been pampering him as he felt a tad more rotund than I remembered. Bribing a cat for loyalty is not a challenging feat though. Cats are food and attention whores.

Vikki and I settled into my living room, and I knew I had to tell her what the attack had washed to the shores of my memories.

"Vikki. There's something I need to tell you."

My story began in 1993.

In a car park in Cheam.

## Chapter Fifty Three

### Cheam concludes

#### 1993

The lights in the car park flickered as the parents awaited their various cares to finish their trampolining lesson. Some were mums, some dads, others were grandparents.

'Or very late starters,' thought Rachel as she viewed the faces massed in front of her. She had been helping her mum coach the trampoline and accompanying gymnastics classes for a year now, as a source of a bit of extra pocket money during her final GCSE year. An avid gymnast herself made for easy work and easier cash, except for a few of the more annoying children though.

One would take forever to get off the trampoline to allow another kid's turn, causing a backlog in the bouncing. By far the best pupil she had was one that almost helped run the class, such was his nature. He was a teaching assistant at this point, and he ensured that there was little to no chaos and fewer calamities caused.

The young boy bounded to her side, looking for his dad's car. He was still feeling the adrenaline from the previous activity so he was active in all his movements.

"Miss Rachel, that's my dad's car. It's very fuel efficient I might add. See? He has the car door open ready." The small boy proclaimed, pointing to the white Ford Escort nestled four cars down. It was still in shadow due to the brilliance of the headlights which shone brightly forward. They seemed to create a wall of light masking the car's interior alongside an annoyance to everyone who glanced in their direction. He assumed that his dad was lost in his comic as he was just as avid a reader as was his son. Rachel nodded to let him know he was cleared to leave her care, but he was already off, having decided it for himself. She smiled warmly at him but was interrupted by another of her wards who stamped on her foot unconsciously as it ran ferally towards a possible parent.

Opening the passenger side door, the boy clambered into the darkened interior but before he could secure the metallic entry again, his senses picked up a foreign smell.

Turning, he saw a mass of grey fur.

Whatever this was, it was facing away from him, concerned with something hidden from view.

Immediately knowing something was wrong, he whimpered and as he did, the beast turned in the car and snarled.

# Chapter Fifty Four

## Nightmares

### 1983

Blood covered the long snout of the wolf in front of Jack who was frozen in both fear and confusion. The scarlet fluid coated teeth as the creature slowly closed the distance to the boy.

Jack noted through his terror that this wolf had silvered orbs for eyes, which swirled and sloshed in its socket. There was no sclera or iris, just a singular silver iris making it impossible to show where its full focus lay through the orb. They had no dark pinprick of direction, but Jack concluded that he was within their aim. He knew this was not something normal in this world, and he tried to comprehend the situation, even though rational thought was failing him.

It sniffed at him.

Licking, at the boy's face. Licking the blood off his snout. It seemed ever hungry, even though there was an acrid, metallic smell in the air.

Jack knew it was the blood. He felt hot fluid in his stomach building, and he knew he was going to be sick.

As the creature drew back, something clicked in Jack's brain, and his naturally logical mind pushed the flee button. Relaxing his arms, he let himself fall backwards out of the passenger door, landing heavily on the ground as the first of the screams filled the car park.

Standing on the opposite side of the car were two feet that Jack could now see from his vantage point at ground level. Another of the leaving children had called to her mother at the sight of the body on the floor.

The body that was Jack's father.

Frustratedly going to see what was stopping them from leaving, she approached her daughter and as she did, became racked with screaming. The sight of the savaged John, his body a mess of rips and tears, was enough to cause the woman to stumble backwards. Her act of scrambling away from the scene brought more attention and yet more screaming.

The vision of the man's face, torn and brutalised, would stay with her forever more, but it was what came next that made her vomit violently.

\*\*\*

The grey fur of the wolf was matted in parts due to the thick viscous blood spouting from various arteries, as it filled its belly. The wolf couldn't remember ever having such a succulent meal before. It had tried different parts of the human, and its mind was dancing between all the various flavours, trying and failing to find its favourite.

A noise behind it focused its attention as a smaller human entered the metal box. Excitedly, it wondered how it would taste. Turning to confront this new youngling, it sniffed at its fresh meal, tasting the air in anticipation of the coming food.

Licking at his face, it tasted the fear it had, and it was oh, so much more deliciously sweeter. Grey moved back on its haunches, preparing to strike and planning to use force of movement to ensure the kill.

It tensed.

It felt the anticipation.

Leaping forward, the boy fell backward but Grey did not care. It had enough momentum to catch the boy when it hit the floor. It was stopped mid-pounce by a hand grabbing its rear leg, pulling it away from the small boy.

With his last breath, John pulled the beast away from his son and back out of the driver's side of the car.

Grey slammed against the parked vehicle and was suddenly aware that groups of humans were looking in its direction.

Fear gripped it.

And with that, Grey ran.

***

The days that followed brought grief, and questions. No one could comprehend what had happened.

Police, with the help of various animal charities, experts, and investigations, found no wolf. None of the sightings could be collaborated with anything evidential, so it was put down to a fox or dog. No one believed it, but it closed the case as a stray dog attack.

Over time, Jack grew to believe the story, his analytical mind forming a logic cage around the terror of that night. He had grieved for years though, forever to miss his loving father.

The night of his dad's death, the young boy had passed out, lost in the grief and emotion of losing your father. Jack's grief was an all-consuming storm that swept through him, relentless and unforgiving. It started with disbelief, a refusal to accept the harsh reality that his dad was gone. He clung to the hope that it was all a terrible mistake, a lie and that his dad would come home. Even if he was weary but alive, and full of stories to tell. Without any sign of his father, the truth settled in like a heavy fog, suffocating and cold.

He awoke that morning in the hospital, as the breeze from a broken window wafted in to cool him.

Every corner of Jack's world felt haunted by memories of his dad. The empty chair at the dinner table, the untouched tools in the shed, the silent echoes of laughter that used to fill their home – They all served as painful reminders of what he had lost. Jack's heart felt like it had been torn apart, each beat a painful reminder of the void his dad's absence had left behind. Anger boiled beneath the surface of Jack's grief; a fierce flame fuelled by the unfairness of it all. Why did it have to be his dad? Why did the wolf have to take him away? He felt a primal urge to lash out, to scream and rail against the cruelty of fate. He learnt how to bottle it up, burying it deep inside where no one could see.

Amid his grief, Jack was lost and adrift, the lights of the emergency service blinding, and the screams of strangers filling his ears.

Amidst all of the pain and confusion, there were moments of bittersweet clarity when Jack felt his dad's presence lingering like a whisper in the wind. He found solace in memories of their time together, in the lessons his dad taught him, and in the love that still bound them transcending even death. Slowly, and painfully, Jack began to navigate the turbulent waters of grief. He learnt quickly how to live with the absence of his dad while cherishing the precious memories they shared. Though the pain never truly faded, it transformed into something softer, a bittersweet ache that served as a testament to the depth of their bond. As Jack walked forward into an uncertain future, he carried his dad's spirit with him, like a guiding light in the darkness.

Even the wound on Jack's leg healed over time.

## Chapter Fifty Five

### Monday...

### Vikki

### 2024

Vikki sat there for a few moments after Jack finished his story, wondering whether to hug him in comfort or love. She chose to do it in both. As she lay against him, careful not to put weight on his injury, questions arose in her that she hadn't had the chance to comprehend. But care rose first, and she hugged him closer.

"Your dad. I'm so sorry." Vikki whispered as tears welled in her eyes. She shuffled closer to him, using connection as a comforter. Moments passed and they both lay there, feeling the love of each other's warmth.

"So, these wolves exist in England? Why haven't there been more deaths? Why haven't we seen them before?" Vikki wanted answers that she was unsure Jack would have the answers to.

"There's a white wolf and a black one?" Her words were left hanging in the air as she lay there, in both fear and worry, craving the safety of Jack's connection. It felt like an hour before either spoke.

"What is the news saying? What's been released to the public?" Jack asked, not having any connection to the media since before the attack. Vikki stayed next to him, but Jack felt her fumbling for her phone, her nails tip-tapping a question into a Google search request. Almost immediately she found a Sky News report about the incident. She read it out to Jack who, when it was finished, pulled Vikki closer to him.

Sky News Report: January 24th, 2024

Reporter: Kay Burley

## Wolf Attack in Epsom, Surrey Leaves One Dead, One Officer Injured

In a shocking incident that has stunned the quiet community of Epsom, Surrey, it was reported that a rare white wolf attacked two individuals yesterday evening, resulting in one fatality and the injury of a responding police sergeant.

The attack occurred around 8 PM in an alleyway leading off the main High Street, an off-street of a popular local spot for shoppers and residents. The victim, identified as 27-year-old local resident Kaleigh Thomas, known commonly as Krystal, was found with severe injuries consistent with a wild animal attack. Despite the best efforts of emergency responders, Ms Thomas was pronounced dead at the scene. Her family has been notified about the details of the victim's death and is being supported by specialist officers.

Authorities were alerted by a distressed passerby who witnessed the attack and called 999. Officers from Surrey Police arrived promptly, attempting to rescue Ms Thomas and contain the situation. During their intervention, one officer sustained injuries from the aggressive animal, believed to be a white wolf, a species not native to the UK. The officer, whose name has not been disclosed, was taken to Epsom General Hospital and is reported to be in stable condition.

The origins of the white wolf remain a mystery, as there have been no recent reports of such animals in the area. Speculation is rife that the animal may have escaped from a private collection or an illegal exotic pet trade operation. Wildlife experts are now involved in the investigation, working to capture the animal and determine its origins.

Epsom residents have been urged to remain vigilant and avoid wooded areas where the wolf is believed to be living until further notice. Surrey Police have set up a dedicated hotline for any sightings or information related to the white wolf.

Chief Inspector Phoebe Darby of Surrey Police addressed the media this morning, expressing condolences to the victim's family and commending the bravery of the injured officer. "This is an unprecedented and tragic event. We are doing everything within our power to ensure the safety of the community, and to apprehend the animals involved. Our thoughts are with Ms. Thomas' loved ones during this difficult time."

Local wildlife rescue organisations have also been mobilised to assist in the search and to offer support to the community. They emphasise the importance of not approaching the animal if spotted and to immediately report any sightings to the authorities.

As the investigation continues, Epsom residents are left grappling with the shock and fear brought by this rare and tragic incident.

Further updates will be provided as more information becomes available, but if you have anything that can assist the investigation, please call 101 quoting reference 7233/23Jan24.

# Chapter Fifty Six

## Wednesday

## Nathan

It had been almost a week since Nathan had seen the wolf, but he'd been following the rolling coverage since its brazen attack. He was livid that their almost thirty years of stealth had been destroyed in a single evening, but more annoyed as he hadn't been there himself to enjoy it.

He would've loved Krystal.

Savoured her.

He felt warmth grow within himself and touched his growing hardness almost unconsciously. She would've made a fine trophy.

Nathan knew something was wrong when he was thrown across the room as if hit by an imaginary car. He lay there for a day, crashed down in the detritus that was his home. The pain and resulting bruise were evidence enough that White had been injured and guessed that he had gone to ground to nurse his wounds. He winced again as both his hip and missing finger pulsed with a reminder of the agony. As the pain in his hand jolted up the nerves in his arm, he tried to think what had happened to White.

He was alive, he knew that otherwise, he wouldn't be. In the days after, he'd healed from both the phantasmal injury and the severed finger. He'd not had to bandage it in a day or so now as the bleeding had stopped. Had been stopped. He'd seen to that by heating a bread knife to the point that it glowed purple and orange, you could use that to sear a wound closed. The pain had ripped through him, almost worse than when the digit was severed, and it had caused him to pass out, but the burn had served its purpose.

"Fuck," he muttered under his breath.

Nathan paced the dimly lit flat, his anger simmering just beneath the surface. His wolf, his other half, had gone rogue, taking down its latest meal solo. The audacity! Nathan would have meticulously planned every detail of their hunts, envisioning the thrill of the kill, the rush of shared glory. Now, White had stolen that moment from him, and while the wolf wouldn't be basking in the limelight as Nathan would be, it was his chance to be seen that was missed. The media buzzed with the story of the ferocious wolf killing the helpless bitch, but Nathan's name was absent, his genius unacknowledged. His presence, unnoticed. The jealousy gnawed at him, each headline a twist of the knife. This wasn't just a betrayal—it was a theft of his identity, his craft. He clenched his fists, vowing that the wolf would pay for this transgression. No one, not even a werewolf, should overshadow Nathan without dire consequences.

He deserved to be noticed.

He wanted to be seen after years in the shadows and this new awakening of violence had been what he was missing in his life.

"You either die a hero or live long enough to see yourself become the villain." Nathan smiled at the quote and marvelled at the irony of Two Face's words. He had two faces himself, but he was no villain. He was the God among men.

"Further updates will be provided as more information becomes available, but if you have anything that can assist the investigation, please call 101 quoting reference 7233/23Jan24." Sky News reported as they moved onto another less depressing topic. Nathan heard the words over and, over in his head, playing them out and he started to construct a new plan.

If he reported the wolf, he'd get the glory with no consequences. He wasn't the owner. He wasn't the killer. He wasn't even there. While the wolf was missing, they couldn't kill it.

All the glory with none of the consequences.

Nathan smiled and picked up the phone.

## Chapter Fifty Seven

### Humanity fails

### Jack

I was finally back at work when I'd heard that a local unit was bringing in a Nathan Greene, (early fifties, white, no warning markers or previous on PNC), for questioning about the wolf attack. We'd been warned that it may have been a wild goose chase, as he was, and I'm quoting the reporting officer here; 'Mad as a box of frogs.' But we needed something to go on. No one had seen or heard anything in relation to the wolf and the tip line was filled with possible sightings in the woods, brief flashes of white fur in the area, and 'it could be my neighbour's Doberman.'

By the time local units had attended any venue though, there was obviously nothing. People were just justifiably on edge.

I know I was. This was a critical incident that would run until we caught the thing. The local press was having a field day. In the week since the attack, they'd moved from 'hero officer' to 'what is being done for public safety?'

Everyone was stressed. We needed something to give out as a positive to people. Policing is twenty percent catching the bad guy and eighty percent trying to get the message out as our day job was often eclipsed as just good news, which didn't sell online blogs or newspapers these days. Give them a bent copper and it was a week's worth of ink, but the media would often fail to note that we'd be more pissed off about that criminal than they were. They'd tarnished our police family.

The radio barked that Nathan had been brought into an interview room and was awaiting a chat with an officer. He hadn't been arrested for anything, even though he'd confirmed that he owned a 'big white wolf.' This needed further investigation and The Dangerous Wild Animals Act 1976 was being poured over for any laws or restrictions broken.

Is owning a wolf in the UK a good idea? No. Is it legal? With a licence, possibly yes... Just, dumb on every level. In my research into this, I found that the 'Government kept a complete list of animals classified as wild that need a licence and must be applied for in the form of The Dangerous Wild Animals Act 1976.' Then I thought 'Why is this even a thing?,' Wild Animals. It's in the bloody title. Wild. People confuse me. Background checks brought up one hit from the night of the incident that Vikki attended and when I mentioned it to her, she immediately brought details flooding back.

The smell. The attitude. The white hair.

She got up to leave as I strode past her, making a beeline for the interview rooms.

## Chapter Fifty Eight

### Making no scents

### Vikki and Nathan

The old police investigation room in Surrey Police's main nick carried an air of history and gravitas, marked by years of service to law enforcement. If you needed to step inside due to being a witness or victim of a crime, the first thing you couldn't fail to notice was the creak of the wooden floorboards beneath your feet. Each step echoed slightly in the quiet room. The walls, once a pristine white, were now yellowed with age. They were adorned with various nicks and scratches, evidence of past confrontations, and countless hours of investigative work.

In the centre of the room stood a sturdy wooden table, its surface marred with scratches and ring stains from countless cups of coffee. The table was flanked by mismatched chairs, some with their original leather upholstery cracked and worn while, others have been reupholstered over the years in a valiant attempt to preserve their usability. The arm of one had been sealed with heavy-duty tape to cover a nasty gouge in the material, but they were generally still as heavy and solid as they were when new in the late eighties. A testament to the era in which they were made when furniture was built to last. Cigarette burns dotted the wood too as haggard detectives of old used to blow acrid smoke in the faces of the guilty and stub their fags out on the wood as a show of force and threat.

Against one wall, an old filing cabinet sat, its metal surface dulled and slightly rusted at the edges. The drawers were labelled with peeling stickers, indicating their contents: "First aid kit," "Crime Prevention Advice Leaflets," "MG11 Witness Statement paper and continuation sheets"

The room was illuminated by a single overhead light fixture, a relic from the mid-20th century, which cast a harsh, bright light that left no shadow unexamined. The fixture occasionally flickered, adding to the room's sense of aged functionality. In one corner, an old radiator clanked intermittently in protest, struggling to provide warmth during the colder months. A large, slightly cracked window offered a view of the bustling streets of Surrey, though its glass distorted the outside world just enough to provide a sense of isolation. The windowsill was cluttered with an assortment of items: an empty coffee cup, an old pen, and a small potted plant that seemed to have been long forgotten, its leaves brown and brittle.

The air in the room carried a mixture of scents: the mustiness of old paper, a hint of fake strawberry from a vape, and the unmistakable smell of stale tobacco from a bygone era when smoking indoors was the norm. The faint aroma of cleaning supplies used in a futile effort to erase the passage of time did little to help the odour. Despite the attempts at cleanliness, the room retained an undeniable sense of wear and tear, a silent witness to the countless hours of intense scrutiny and critical decision-making that took place within its walls. This old police investigation room, with its palpable sense of history, stood as a testament to the tireless efforts of those who have worked to solve crimes and bring justice to the community of Surrey.

In one of the chairs sat Nathan. Vikki clocked the same level of eerie disarrangement, his rumpled clothes the same as that fateful night. He emanated the distinct, pungent odour of a dog as if he had spent significant time in close quarters with them. With it.

The scent mingled with the faint mustiness of the room, creating an almost tangible atmosphere of tension and discomfort. Nathan's eyes moved up and down Vikki, who was now in official CID clothing, taking in a form hidden under the confines of a police uniform.

He leered up at her and smiled, as the sound of a distant howl filled the night air.

# Chapter Fifty Nine

## The grand reveal

## The Wolf

The moon hung high and full over the woodland, casting its silver luminescence across the dense foliage. The trees stood tall and silent, their leaves rustling softly in the night breeze. Within this nocturnal tranquillity, a shadow moved swiftly, its form blending seamlessly with the surrounding darkness.

White's fur shimmered under the moonlight, and its eyes glowed with otherworldly intensity. After its stomach had been filled with human nourishment, it had been a freeing feeling that surged power through White's veins. It was intoxicating to the beast, who wanted more; however, in the aftermath of his recent meal, his eyes were filled with pain and desperation.

The wolf had run from the police car that had smashed into its flank and lost the humans that were chasing it by disappearing into a local wood. The impact had been brutal. The car's headlights illuminated the wolf for a split second before it was sent sprawling onto the asphalt, a howl of its agony piercing the night.

The officers, terrified and confused, had seen only a large, white animal before it scrambled into the nearby woods, leaving a trail of blood in its wake.

As White hid, deep in the heart of the forest, the werewolf lay hidden in a thicket, its body battered, but not broken. It had managed to run away from the scene, instincts guiding it to a place where it could heal away from prying eyes. The werewolf's injuries were severe – a fractured rib, a deep gash along its side, and a limp in its left hind leg that made every step an excruciating effort.

For the first few days, the werewolf's existence was a blur of pain and feverish dreams. It lay on a bed of leaves and moss, barely able to move, its breath coming in shallow, laboured gasps. The forest provided some comfort, the familiar scent and sound soothing its agitated mind. Birds chirped during the day, and nocturnal creatures rustled in the underbrush at night, a reminder that life continued even as it fought to survive.

The healing process would have been slow had the wolf been a normal one, this werewolf's supernatural regenerative abilities were formidable, even though the severity of its injuries required time. Each day brought improvement. The werewolf's rib began to mend, the deep gash closed, and the limp, while still painful, became less pronounced.

The forest itself seemed to aid in the healing. White found a small stream where he could drink and clean its wounds. The cool, clear water was a balm to its injuries, and the surrounding plants provided medicinal herbs that it instinctively used to speed the recovery. The werewolf chewed on certain leaves to ease the pain and rolled crushed herbs into its wounds to stave off infection.

As the week progressed, the werewolf's strength returned, only hindered by one day when a stabbing burning pain racked up his leg, as if scolded by a red-hot piece of metal.

It ventured further from its makeshift den, testing its healed body. Each step, each movement, was a triumph over the pain that had threatened to overwhelm it, and the wolf pushed on, hunting small game. As it ate it was regaining energy and muscle mass, the taste of fresh meat revitalising it.

On the seventh night, under the light of the full moon, the werewolf stood at the edge of the forest, looking out at the world it had briefly encountered. The memory of the police car and the pain it had inflicted was still vivid, a reminder of the dangers that lurked in the human world. The werewolf was not deterred. It was stronger now, both physically and mentally, having survived the ordeal and emerged resilient.

The werewolf let out a long, haunting howl that echoed through the forest, a declaration of its survival and strength. It now needed to find its human host as together they'd always been strong.

It needed its half; it could sense where it was.

It instinctively moved to be by his side.

## Chapter Sixty

### The Watcher's confession

### Vikki and Nathan

Vikki could feel Nathan's eyes upon her. She likened it to dripping oil on your skin, such was the oozing gaze she felt. She took a deep breath, steeling herself for the upcoming interview. She'd offered to take the lead on the flights down and Jack had agreed, knowing her line of questioning would be more accurate than his. He had skin in this game and Vikki wanted to give him distance, both emotionally and professionally. She regretted it almost immediately as Nathan ran eyes all over her. Witness interviews were part of the job, but dealing with lecherous men was an unfortunate, uncomfortable aspect she had grown to despise. Every flick of his eyes raked over her in a way that made her skin crawl.

"Good evening. Mr Nathan Greene, isn't it? How's the hand? Better I hope." The question was designed to distract him while also offering some care to the wound he received. "Mr. Greene, I'm Detective Constable Victoria Doherty and I hear you know about the wolf that was loose in the town centre?" She made sure to keep her tone professional, her expression neutral, even though every muscle wanted, craved to punch him in the face. His demeanour cried out for him to be hit. Hard. With a bat.

"Of course, Vikki, I know everything. I like your name by the way. I like the feel of it on my tongue." he replied, his voice oozing with an attempt at charm. "Please, call me Nathan. Or Nath. Whichever you love more." He smiled and leaned forward in his chair, ignoring the normal etiquette of the rest of the planet's residents.

"Thank you, Nathan," Vikki said, ignoring his advances, while suppressing a shiver at the thought. She chose a seat opposite him so that the table blocked the view and gave distance between them, as Jack moved to stand in the corner of the room. She took out her notepad and pen as Nathan moved in his chair. He had placed his feet wide, one either side of Vikki's, making no effort to maintain a respectable distance.

"So, Detective Vikki," he said, leaning in, "Where do you want me to start?" Vikki forced a smile, focusing on the task at hand, and trying not to meet his wandering eyeline.

"I'd like to ask you a few questions about the incident on Tuesday the 23rd of January involving the wolf attack on Ms. Thomas. You claimed on the 101 call to have knowledge about the wolf?" The strength it took to recall the details was still traumatic. Every time she closed her eyes, she saw the wolf biting down on her Jack. The memory caused her to grip her pen tightly, her hand whitening under her exerted pressure.

"Ah, yes, that night." Nathan's eyes glinted as he spoke, his gaze lingering on her longer than necessary. "I remember it well. But before we get into that, can I have a drink? I'll take a tea or coffee. Or something stronger if you want? Go fetch." He gestured with his hand for Jack to leave but the younger sergeant stood motionless, not allowing the rudeness to rise him.

"No, we don't have facilities for that," Vikki replied firmly. "Let's stick to the matter at hand."

Nathan sighed dramatically and leaned back in his

chair, his eyes fixed on Jack. He settled back into his chair but was still close enough that Vikki could feel his presence looming over her.

"As you wish, Detective. So forceful. I like that in a woman. So, what first then?" At the last words, Jack took a step towards Nathan, but out of sight, Vikki motioned for him to calm down and he returned to his leaning position in the corner.

"You mentioned having information about the wolf. Is it yours? Do you own it?" Vikki tried to keep Nathan on track, but she noticed he was revelling in the attention. Nathan's eyes wandered to her chest before he looked up at her face again, a slow smile spreading across his lips.

"Of course, I know about it. It's part of me." At the sound of the words, his grin spread across his face, baring teeth in a smile born of mania. Jack and Vikki stared at him, his words not fully computing.

"Sorry, Mr Greene, can you explain that?" Vikki said as Nathan leaned in closer, his breath unpleasantly warm against her cheek. She clenched her jaw, resisting the urge to snap, as Nathan chuckled, clearly enjoying her discomfort and confusion.

"I am the White Wolf. We are as one." His words hung in the air and Nathan turned his gaze to Jack. "You know what I'm talking about don't you?"

Vikki stood up abruptly, needing to put physical distance between herself and Nathan. "Thank you for your time, Mr. Greene, you are clearly not going to be helpful in our investigation. I will get an officer to take you home if one is available."

Nathan stood as well, leaning in closer than necessary over the table. Jack moved to her side and this time; she didn't stop him.

"But don't you want to hear about the other werewolf?"

## Chapter Sixty One

### From White to Black

### Jack

At this point, I took over the interview. I hated the way this individual was talking to, talking at, my staff, my Vikki.

"Talk." It wasn't as professional as I'd wanted, but at this point, I just wanted the details. We needed to know what the hell was going on. Wolves, a missing young person, a dead woman. I needed to know where this was going. For the investigation and myself. Nathan was smiling broadly now, clearly enjoying the attention and control.

"So, you know the legend. Silver bullets, changing at the full moon, American Werewolf in London. It is all complete bollocks. All these films, books, and terrible tales you tell your kids at night, they're all based on something. Everything always is." Smiling further still, he continued, his grin tinged with a manic delight. "Werewolves are born from humans; they are part of the same being. My wolf is out there right now, healing from the wounds that you bastards did. Ask me how I know this. Go on, I dare you." He was goading me, I knew it, but I had to let the information, however shit, flow.

I motioned for him to continue with a wave of my hand, still unsure how much bollocks this twat was going to vomit up. I gave him the nod, not wanting to waste oxygen on calling forth the words. Something inside me though, urged me to listen as if this was information long overdue.

"You must've hit him with a car or something, yes? On his side?" He asked, wanting to know but seemingly knowing already. We hadn't released that to the public, so this was going to be interesting. We'd made sure to canvas everyone in the area and speak to every witness, and this person in my interview room was not one of them that the investigating officers named. The team could've missed him, with all the chaos, it could've been a possibility. I say we... I was sparked out on pain meds by that point.

Nathan sat slowly and Vikki moved herself back in her chair, to give her more distance from the lecherous male. Space was also an 'officer safety' standard as an unknown person could lash out wildly due to their mental state, alcohol or drug consumption, or just that they were an arsehole. I kept my ground though purely because I didn't want to give this idiot even more control than he already had.

He began raising his shirt on the right-hand side. Down his rib cage was the healed remnant of a bruise. As if he'd been run over. The large bruise looked to be about a week old (that tracked) as it resembled an abstract painting, its hues shifting and blending in a mesmerising array. At its core, the bruise was a deep, stormy purple, akin to the rich tones of a midnight plum, still holding onto the trauma that birthed it. Surrounding this heart of darkness, the colour faded into a bruised maroon, like the deep, velvety petals of a wilting rose. As the bruise stretched outward, it transitioned into an angry red, reminiscent of sunset clouds on a turbulent evening, hinting at the inflammation that once was.

It was as if he'd been hit by a car.

Vikki was lost in thought, her mind calculating. Mine on the other hand was awash with theories of how and why and coming up with nothing. I didn't want another unsolvable case on my hands, as they would both plague me. Nathan was smiling at us through the crook of his arm.

I'd known about the wolves, but werewolves? It was quickly becoming too much, and I wanted to ground this with some solid science. But deep down?

"And you got this when?" I said, already knowing what his gloat-filled answer would be. I had taken an instant dislike to this cockwomble. I motioned for him to sit as the movement of his shirt wafted a scent into the room no one ever needed to smell. It was as if Lynx created a deodorant called 'death and depression.' Thankfully he did, but the smell lingered, like a bad Nathan.

"To clarify. You are 'linked' to this white wolf, and you share the same damage? So, it will be missing a finger too?" I said, motioning to his hand. "My colleague came to a call the night of the wolf attack and said that you were nursing an injury. How did that happen?" This time, control was mine.

"We had a disagreement. White bit it off. He lost one at the same time though, so I hope it was worth it. Same body, remember. It gets wounded, so do I, and vice versa. It dies, I die." I'll give him one thing, he himself believed what he was saying. There was no deviation from the same tale. There was normally some sign that gave away that there was a mental health condition at play. A person with delusions would often feed into narratives, and you could add jigsaw pieces to their puzzled minds, which they would lap up and add to their stories like they were being given credibility.

"How did you…" I checked my meagre notes, all of

which were bullet points "How is the wolf born from you? You know that's not scientifically possible, yes?" I needed to add in some science as this was going way off track. Nathan unfortunately had an answer though.

"I got bit. Walking home in Cheam in the nineties, this grey wolf flew out of the alleyway to some school and launched itself at me. Fucker took a chunk out of my ear as he ran off too."

His words broke me as memories flooded back.

A grey wolf. In Cheam. In the nineties.

The same one that killed my dad.

The same one that bit me.

At that point, all three of us heard the sound of shattering glass from somewhere deeper in the building.

## Chapter Sixty Two

### Incoming

### The Wolf

The night was unsettlingly quiet, the kind of stillness that precedes a storm. The police station, bathed in the cold glow of fluorescent lights, buzzed with the low hum of routine activity. Officers sifted through paperwork, phones rang intermittently, and the scent of stale coffee lingered in the air. The ground floor writing room was abuzz with officers catching up on paperwork as the window shattered into the room. Glass shards lacerated arms and tore through whatever exposed skin it touched; such was the ferocity of the impact. Everyone turned to see the shattering as the mass of white fur flew through the broken frame.

A large wolf landed amongst them, with an audible thwump of paws on the floor. It was without any warning, the relative tranquillity of a police station shattered by an explosion of glass. The monstrous lupine figure was now bathed by the strip lighting above, showing the officer how enormous it was. Its fur was a stark white that seemed to glow under the artificial lights, its eyes blazing with a predatory intensity.

Panic immediately erupted through the gathered officers, most of whom were not in their body armour, or had any protective equipment to hand. Some ran. Some froze. Some grabbed for their radio to jab at the 'Emma' button, hoping that the emergency signal would be heard by everyone. What they could do though was unknown, but the cry for help was an unconscious yelp when needed.

Chaos erupted in that instant. Desks were overturned as officers scrambled for anything they could use as a weapon, their training battling with sheer terror. The wolf moved with feral speed and power, a blur of fur and claws. Its growls reverberated through the station, a primal sound that froze the blood of anyone who heard it.

The first officer to confront the beast was thrown aside with a swipe of its massive head, his body slamming into a wall with bone-crushing force. The air was filled with shouts and the deafening cacophony of all their radios asking 'what the hell was going on' in unison. No weapons seemed worthy. An old chair was used as a makeshift shield, but the wolf seemed unstoppable, as it was driven by an unholy rage and resilience.

Another officer was caught in its deadly embrace, the wolf's jaws snapping shut with a sickening crunch. Blood sprayed across the room, painting the walls in a macabre red. The scent of blood thickened in the air, mingling with the acrid tang of fear.

Amid the pandemonium, the creature's objective remained clear: it was clear to all officers left standing that it was searching for something or someone. It moved with purpose, its snarls and howls echoing down the corridors. Desperate cries for backup filled the airwaves, as the station became a battlefield, and the officers within were trapped in a nightmare.

In the flickering lights, the scene was a blur of movement and violence, a harrowing tableau of human fragility against primal savagery. The wolf's path of destruction was a gruesome reminder of the thin line between order and chaos, a line that had been violently breached by a force of nature that defied comprehension.

The wolf leapt towards the corridor and stopped at a young police community support officer who was frozen in place. White had entered the room at the same time as the PCSO, who was now barring the wolf's path. He tried to calm the beast, but nothing was going to stop it from reuniting with Nathan. The staff officer was knocked over with the force of the wolf's jump and landed heavily on his back.

White took the opportunity to raise the chaos levels by biting clean through the PCSO's neck, severing it to the spine. Blood jutted everywhere as arteries were torn through, the fountain covering another nearby police officer. This officer, a woman in her forties, collapsed screaming in a heap, unable to process the horror in front of her. Blood dripped down her face, and she blinked rapidly as it dripped into her eyes, the feeling of the gore making her retch and vomit into her lap. She lost further control when the PCSOs head lolled backwards at an impossible angle as the normal muscle and sinews holding it upright were being chewed by the rampaging wolf.

The smell in the air became overpowering. Blood. Vomit. Urine.

White felt the power it had and was relishing in it.

Proceeding down the corridor, the wolf came to the door to a small office, and his keen hearing could hear whimpering from the other side. Someone was hiding there that was a distraction to its quest to find his host, but White took the time to raise itself against the door. Looking through the glass window, White saw a woman, hiding behind a collection of computers and screens.

The wolf licked against the glass, leaving a blood smear in its wake. The wolf realised how much he was enjoying the smell of fear coming from these humans. It smelt of power and made the beast feel alive like never before.

The wolf moved further down the corridor, leaving the woman screaming and alone. He followed the presence of its host and wanted nothing more than to be with him now. He knew that they were better together, better as one. He also knew that his actions a week ago had caused him to be wounded, and that was something that he'd never had to deal with when he was by the side of his host.

They'd be together again, and they'd be free to do as they pleased now. They would kill and hunt like the apex predators they were.

The white wolf was metres from the interview room door.

## Chapter Sixty Three

### No threat to me

### Jack

"Told you we were one," Nathan said, letting out a cackle of power towards us. I was struggling to hold it together as this person was somehow connected to my greatest loss. Vikki had clocked it too and I could see the concern in her eyes. She knew what this must be doing to me, so took back over, to give me time to reset myself, to draw a breath that I hadn't realised I was holding.

We'd both heard the crash and initially thought it was a glass or some other crockery being dropped, then the screams afterwards brought a fear we always felt. Something was wrong, and it was down to us all, the police family, to sort it out.

Nathan was still smiling although it had turned darker, more devious.

"What's happening Nathan? You know something." Vikki said with the strength that belied her small frame. She was on her feet now, taking charge of the situation as police do. I wasn't helping. I was stuck on his words. I could barely move. A scrape of something against the door broke this frailty that had gripped me. It was reminiscent of a dog clawing at a door to come in. A dog. Or a wolf. Moving quickly, I lifted the large wooden table and slid it across the floor. I wedged it against the door as the first thud hit it from the corridor. Nathan was still sitting in the seat he occupied but had taken a relaxed stance, his legs wide, in a dominant posture.

Another thud.

Another.

Something definitely wanted in, and I couldn't see it from the window in the wooden door. I didn't need any evidence though, it was the white wolf, and it had come for its master, host or whatever Nathan was. Somehow, with everything that had happened, I knew that all this was somehow true.

Ghosts exist. Werewolves exist.

Both kill.

I resigned myself to relook at my entire life's direction if we got through this. I wondered briefly what came next, but right now though, we needed an out, but all I could think of was 'What else is out there?'

"Vikki, hold this table!" I ordered, not feeling we had the time to plan. She moved into action after the last word and did as ordered. Swapping, I picked up her chair and flung it through the window, thankful that our building was as ancient as it was. I winced in pain as the effort sent an electric wave jolting through my arm, a reminder of the healing injury. We needed to leave now, to put distance between us and the wolf so that we could call in trained reinforcements.

Another thud. A splintering of old wood.

"Vikki, get out, I'll hold the table. Nathan, I suggest you follow her." I was in full tactician mode now. Protect people. Stop them getting hurt. Even the bad ones. But Nathan was still smiling, still sitting.

Thud… Thud… An audible crack. The glass of the viewing window spiderwebbed upwards like lightning from the ground. Thankfully, the metal lattice embedded in the glass was holding it mostly in place.

"He's no threat to me. It's you he wants. He can smell it on you." Everything he said was weird and creepy and gross, even to me and I didn't have time to psychoanalyse him at this point. Vikki was out, into the yard beyond and I could see officers readying everything they could. There was a clamour unlike any I'd seen before. To the untrained eye, it looked like unprofessional chaos, but to mine, I knew what everyone was defaulting to. Yet, there was still an obvious glint of fear in everyone's eyes.

Fear that they'd lost some of their police family.

I had a choice to make. I could either leave Nathan here or try and throw him outside. This brought the risk that he truly believed his words and would fight back, thus creating a greater risk for me. One last try.

"Nathan! OUT!" I thought that the force of my words would determine my next actions, but it was Nathans. He was laughing.

Turning, I leapt through the window and into the yard as the door burst inwards.

# Chapter Sixty Four

## More wolves

### Black

The black wolf paced. It had missed the chance to help his host having been too far away from the incident, and now, though close, knew it was too exposed to help. The logical part of its mind that it had been gifted from its host had made the hard decision not to step in. Yet Black's heart screamed against the idea.

He would be no help dead and there were far too many people around to risk it.

Black watched with piercing silver eyes, hidden close enough to act, but out of any of the sightlines of the human world. He'd chosen a particularly shadowy part of an old oak tree so he could monitor his host, the one called Jack. He'd been born in secret to a young boy and had left his side as there would be chaos and panic if his parent woke the next morning to find a large black wolf by his side. He'd chosen to watch from afar. It was logical. Stay hidden, and they would both stay safe.

The police station was teeming with people, running around with the urgency of emergency. Black's heart raced with a mix of anxiety and determination. He wanted to be there, by his host's side, or better still, in front, protecting him, and his mate. The large wolf's senses were bringing information to him that the humans would be missing. He could feel the White one and its host together in a room, and then making their escape in the cacophony of chaos the wolves' murdering spree had caused. His keen eyes followed Jack as he navigated through the police crowd, always keeping him in sight. The hill gave an excellent vantage point into the backyard and the tree the sanctity of stealth. Jack's movements were purposeful, showing the leader he was. He was getting units organised, but some kept back at a distance away from where he last saw the white wolf. Black had learned to remain hidden, to avoid drawing attention to himself, but his every instinct screamed to be by Jack's side, to protect him from any harm.

As the minutes ticked agonisingly by, Black's apprehension grew. He knew that the white wolf and host were long gone now, and the officers were attending to their injured and dead.

His sharp nose caught a scent that made his hackles rise – the faint trace of wolf and adrenaline. He knew that smell all too well; it was the scent of impending danger. His muscles coiled, ready to spring into action, but the mass of people made any overt move impossible. A large black wolf in Epsom Town Centre would cause panic and chaos, blowing any chance of helping Jack and endangering countless lives.

From his vantage point, Black could trace the hidden steps of the wolf. Knowing Jack was currently safe from harm, he followed his nose, wanting nothing more than to kill one of the pair that had done so much damage. So many dead. He knew he only needed to kill one of them and the other half would die also. Such was their symbiotic relationship. Killing the man would by far be easier, but Black wanted to kill the wolf more. Even though they were as one, killing the man still offended his sense of morality. Black's heart pounded as he went through tactical options. He had to act, but he needed to do so without causing alarm to the populace. He darted along the perimeter of the wooded area, keeping the smell of the white strong in his nostrils. He moved with purpose, and with the silent grace of a shadow, every muscle in his body honed for this moment.

The black wolf moved with lethal grace, his sleek form a shadow against the concrete and brick. His eyes, fierce and unwavering, locked onto the figure of the white wolf ahead, a stark contrast to the night. The thrill of the hunt coursed through his veins, a primal energy that heightened his senses and sharpened his focus. Every muscle in his body coiled and released with precision, propelling him in a silent, relentless pursuit. The white wolf could have been just as aware of the predator on his heels, but Black was adept at being the shadow he'd always lived in. He darted through alleys and leapt over obstacles, silent in every stride. The black wolf's breath came in steady, controlled bursts, each exhale a testament to his determination. The air was thick with tension, the clamour of the police station now far behind him. These new streets though, bore witness to an ancient dance of predator and prey, where instinct and cunning dictated every move. The hunt was not just a chase; it was a battle of wills, a test of endurance and strategy, and the black wolf relished every moment of it. As Black neared the pair, who were now making their way into an old storefront, a growl rumbled deep in his throat, but he held it back. He needed the perfect moment. It would happen, he'd save Jack and his mate too. He cared for both now as they were his family, albeit from afar.

She needed protecting too.

Her, and her baby.

## Chapter Sixty Five

So... many... dead...

Jack and Vikki

Vikki was covered in blood. Not her own, which was somehow worse. She'd rather it had been and not the police officer choking on his punctured lung. He was looking up at her imploring her to save him as she applied pressure to a terminal wound. There was desperation and realisation in his eyes as an ambulance team arrived to take over from her.

She'd never seen so many officers. Armed response teams were here, as were all the dog units she'd ever encountered. 'This would end tonight one way or another' she thought, hoping for it, but needing revenge for all these dead.

Seven dead.

The other seriously injured all had life-changing or threatening wounds. None were believed to get through the next hour. 'This wolf thing, whatever it was, had torn its way through our police family' was all that went through Vikki's mind.

The aftermath of the attack on their police station, their home, was a scene of chaotic devastation. The window of entry was shattered as was their exit point, but inside, the carnage was extensive. Inner doors, now splintered and hanging off their hinges, bore deep claw marks and gouges, evidence of the ferocity of the assault. Inside, the writing room was in an earthquake level of disarray: overturned chairs, shattered glass from the broken window, and papers were strewn across the floor like fallen leaves. The air was thick with the acrid scent of fear and adrenaline, mingling with the metallic tang of blood from officers who had attempted to fend off the beast.

Desks were toppled, computers lay in ruin, their screens cracked and flickering with static. Walls, once pristine, were marred by deep scratches, and the occasional bloody handprint told of desperate struggles. Officers, bruised and bandaged, moved about with grim determination, their faces etched with a mix of shock and resolve. They spoke in hushed tones, piecing together the chaotic events of the attack, their voices echoing in the now eerily quiet station. The threatening, mournful growl of the wolf seemed to linger in the air, a haunting reminder of the terror that had swept through the station. One officer was vomiting nothing as his stomach had been spent long ago.

Outside, the flashing lights of many police pandas bathed the scene in a surreal, strobing glow, casting long shadows that danced across the building's facade. The streets outside were also cordoned off, coloured bright red and blue from the silent lights atop many of the police cars. Curious onlookers were kept at bay by solemn-faced officers, each trying to hold what they had together. Some failed and burst into tears, to be caught by both a fellow officer and the quick hands of a person's mobile phone. The scent of fear lingered, mixing with the earthy smell of the night, as the police of Epsom tried to come to terms with the unimaginable attack by a creature that seemed to have stepped out of legend.

Looking around, Vikki saw Jack was already armoured over his plain clothes, and also heavily blood-stained.

He was arguing with a senior officer about not being assigned to the search. Jack was having none of it and told the Inspector that nothing would stop him from helping his fallen brothers and sisters. Vikki smiled. She loved this ferocity in him.

Their conversation was brought to an abrupt halt when an ambulance team brought out another stretcher. Jack moved directly to its side, and she saw immediate pain in his eyes. Rushing to his side, she heard the words of the injured officer, through gargled blooded pain.

"I tried..."

Jim was rushed into the back of an ambulance and away as Jack stood there. His fists were clenched to white, the force giving them a shudder that only abject anger caused. He looked back at the inspector, which was part threat, part defiance.

"Go. Authorised." He returned, as the senior officer realised that his sergeant would do what he wanted with or without authority. He knew he would do the same thing if roles were reversed. Everyone would. No one could sit by and watch this pass by...

"Vikki, get armoured up, we're going to find Nathan."

\*\*\*

I was a mix of all the emotions I had squashed down. Fear, anger, and revenge were joined with an impotence of how I could keep everyone safe. Standing in the rear yard of our police station, that I called home and seeing it like this, it downright crushed me. The station was in shambles, a twisted echo of the place I had walked into every shift morning for the last year. My hands trembled as I tried to bring some order to the chaos, picking up shattered pieces of glass and splintered wood, the remnants of what used to be a writing desk. How parts of it were now in the back yard was beyond my comprehension at this point. I didn't know if I was going to try and fix it at this point, such was the confusion racing through me. The injured officers were all away to the various hospitals and the dead were all covered, yet the metallic scent of blood and the acrid stench of fear still hung in the air, almost suffocating me. I couldn't breathe. I had to.

The small yellow markers dotted around signifying evidence resembled tiny tombstones and officers moved around them in the same daze as I was now filled with. Some PCs were trying to attend to the minor wounded who were refusing help so that they could help others, while others were securing the broken premises.

All of them had the same haunted look in their eyes.

I knew that everyone depended on me. I gulped down a lungful of much-needed air and dropped the shards onto the ground. I felt like screaming out at the top of my lungs in sheer, vengeful anger, and while I thought it might have helped me and others, I bottled it down. I had to show strength to my team, and my family. They needed leadership and guidance so that they would avenge their fallen. I took it all on my shoulders at that minute. This was now all my responsibility, to hell with rank.

I felt the weight of responsibility pressing down on me, it was my job now after all. It was on me. It became a crushing force that I felt deep within. My shoulders began aching from the weight of this new world. I had taken it all on my shoulders, the aftermath of the wolf's attack, the destruction, the terror. Every cry for help, every report of the injured, every panicked call from my friends echoed in my mind. I was their sergeant; they looked to me for leadership, for strength, and I couldn't let them down. But inside, I was fraying at the edges, barely holding it all together.

I glanced around, my eyes seeking out familiar faces. It was then that I truly saw her – Vikki. Her usually composed demeanour was marred by a hint of worry. Her eyes scanned the wreckage until they locked onto mine. She must have seen the struggle in my face, the way my hands shook despite my efforts to steady them. Her presence was a beacon of calm in the storm that raged around us.

"Vikki… I said…" my voice was breaking, wavering as I tried to report the request. "You need your vest on. We're going to find Nathan."

She didn't respond. She was moving closer to me, her movements purposeful and yet gentle, a stark contrast to the chaos that surrounded us. My heart ached at the sight of her, a painful reminder of the love I had kept hidden, the love that now felt more vulnerable than ever amidst the ruin of our world.

"Jack," she said softly, her voice cutting through the noise and the panic. "You're doing everything you can. We'll get through this."

I tried to respond, to put on a brave face, but the words caught in my throat. The weight of the situation, the fear of failing those who depended on me, it was all too much. Tears I had been holding back threatened to spill over.

She reached out, her hand resting on my arm, a touch that was both grounding and electrifying. "Jack," she repeated, her voice firmer now. "You don't have to do this alone."

Before I could react, she closed the distance between us, her lips meeting mine in a kiss that was as unexpected as it was needed. At that moment, the chaos faded into the background. The broken glass, the blood, the fear – it all melted away, leaving just the two of us standing there, bathed in the red and blue lights. Her kiss was a lifeline, a reminder that I wasn't alone in this battle, that someone cared deeply for me, and that I was loved. It was a strong, primitive wave of emotion which engrossed my senses in a deluge of love. It was all that a human could possibly want. To be for someone.

I kissed her back, my hands finding her waist, pulling her closer. Nothing else mattered, everything else was silent. It was a kiss filled with unspoken promises, with a desperate need for connection amidst the destruction. When we finally pulled apart, her forehead rested against mine, and I could see the resolve in her eyes.

"We'll get through this," she repeated, her voice a whisper now, just for me. "Together."

I took a deep breath, feeling some of the weight lift from my shoulders. She was right. We would get through this, not because I was a sergeant trying to hold everything together on my own, but because we were a team. And we had each other.

I nodded, a renewed sense of determination filling me. "Together," I echoed.

As we stood there, amidst the wreckage and the

chaos, I felt a spark of hope ignite within me. We will rebuild, we will heal, and we will face whatever comes next, side by side.

We will find the white wolf.

It was our turn to hunt.

# Chapter Sixty Six

## Predators and prey

## Nathan and White

Nathan stood at the grimy window of a run down shop, peering through a crack in the dusty blinds. The streets of the small town in Surrey were eerily quiet now, the aftermath of chaos settling like a heavy fog. A triumphant smile played on his lips as he glanced at the white wolf lying calmly by the door. The wolf's pristine fur was marred by flecks of dirt and blood, trophies from his daring assault on the police station.

The shop they had taken refuge in was a forgotten relic of a bygone era, once a thriving greengrocer's but now a shell of its former self. Dust-covered shelves stood empty, their contents long since pilfered or decayed. The walls, once bright with cheerful paint, were now faded and peeling, revealing patches of bare plaster underneath. Broken tiles littered the floor, and the air was thick with the musty smell of neglect and abandonment.

Nathan felt a surge of pride and exhilaration. He'd felt seen finally as his plan had worked out perfectly. He could still hear the panicked shouts of the officers, the sound of glass shattering, and the growls of his loyal companion echoing in his mind. The fear they had sown was palpable, and it filled him with a sense of power and control.

For too long, he had been hidden, held back by the fear of being caught. However tonight, he had struck back with a force they would not soon forget.

They would never forget him and the power he held.

The wolf, his eyes a piercing silver, gazed up at Nathan with a look of understanding and loyalty. They were tinged with an apology for the attack days earlier, but all had been forgiven, as Nathan felt for the first time, the life he'd always dreamed of. The life he was owed. After everything it had thrown at him, now was his time.

He knelt, ruffling the fur around the wolf's neck. "You did well, boy," he whispered, his voice tinged with admiration. White had been his constant companion through thick and thin, a fierce protector and an even fiercer weapon. Together, they had become a force to be reckoned with.

The shop's backroom served as their temporary hideout. An old, battered mattress lay in one corner, its springs creaking under Nathan's weight as he sat down. He reached into a bag he'd stashed there before his trip to the station and pulled out a small stash of supplies: a few cans of food, a bottle of water, and a first-aid kit. They would need to move again soon, but for now, they could rest and regroup.

White had food too.

When they'd arrived, a homeless drunk was just about to rifle through the bag, but Nathan had moved quickly, grabbing him around the throat. He'd used his newfound strength to choke the man into unconsciousness as White watched on. This would be his first actual kill, and he wanted to prove to the great wolf that he had it in him too. He would also offer it to him to feed and empower. An offering from God to God.

Nathan's mind raced with plans for their next move. The police would be on high alert, searching for any sign of them, but he had always been good at staying one step ahead. He could blend into the shadows, disappearing into the night with White by his side. They would find another target, strike again, and remind those in power that they were invincible. Power was with the Were's now. He was one of the oldest. He wasn't going to instigate any of the 'Alpha wolf' bollocks, but they would respect him as one. He would kill any that stood against him.

He glanced around the dimly lit room, noting the remnants of the shop's past. A rusted cash register sat atop the counter; its keys frozen in time. Old posters advertising fresh produce clung to the walls, their colours faded and edges curling. The large display window at the front was cracked, a spiderweb of fractures distorting the view of the street outside.

As the night deepened, Nathan listened to the distant sounds of the town: the occasional car passing by, the muffled voices of late-night wanderers, and the rustle of leaves in the wind. In this moment of quiet triumph, he felt a bond with White that was deeper than what they had before. They were more than just man and beast; they were a team, united in their defiance and their quest for freedom, and power.

The shop's disrepair mirrored the life Nathan had now left behind – a life of confinement, of being told where to go and what to do. Now, he was free, living on his terms, with his wolf as his only true companion. The thrill of their recent victory fuelled his resolve. They would continue their journey, always moving forward, always staying ahead of those who sought to cage them.

Nathan lay back on the mattress, closing his eyes and listening to White's steady breathing. Tomorrow would bring new challenges, but tonight, they could bask in the glory of their triumph. In this forgotten corner of Surrey, hidden away from prying eyes, Nathan and his white wolf had found a fleeting moment of peace and victory.

# Chapter Sixty Seven

## Hunting

### Jack

Everyone standing was now out of the station. It was our turn to hunt. No stone would be left unturned and if a door would be knocked in with our big red key, the force used would be as therapeutic as it was kinetic. Teams from other forces had joined us to help as they all felt the same pain. This was an attack on all our hearts, and we screamed and searched as one.

I had taken my team to canvas the area around Nathan's home with an armed response as a local backup. We knocked on everyone's door, and politeness was a lost concept. We were down to 'yes and no' answers now, such was our need to find Nathan and his fucking wolf. I knew he wouldn't be here but it gave me great pleasure to kick his door down with one swift kick. It stunk inside. How anyone could or would want to live in such a shit hole was beyond me. The 'home' in inverted commas was an absolute catastrophe, a nauseating cesspool of filth and decay. The front door, now off its hinges, lay amidst the chaotic, cluttered interior. The air inside was thick with the stench of rotting food and unwashed bodies, mingling with the sharp, acrid odour of urine and wet dog fur. An officer vomited in the hallway due to the wave of disgusting odour that wafted out.

As I stepped inside, the first thing that hit me was the overwhelming sight of garbage strewn across every surface. Empty food containers, takeout boxes, and drink cans were scattered haphazardly, many overturned and spilling their rancid contents onto the floor. The lino was sticky underfoot and stained with God only knows what. The living room was a minefield of discarded clothing, tattered and stained with no one wanting to know what. It was piled high in corners, draped over furniture and even the sofa. This would have once been a soft, inviting place to sit, now a sagging wreck, its upholstery was torn and gnawed at, likely by the resident wolf. Dirty, threadbare blankets and pillows were heaped on it, some covered in patches of fur and dried drool.

Everything in here went against everything I was. Where I was calm and collected, this was the anti-Jack. I forced myself to look around for anything of note, any evidence that I could use to aid the search. Fuck it. To aid the cunt hunt. In one corner, an old television flickered intermittently, surrounded by a sea of beer bottles and ashtrays overflowing with cigarette ends. The coffee table was buried under layers of junk mail, unopened bills, and remnants of half-eaten meals. The surfaces were sticky, and the smell of stale tobacco permeated the air.

The kitchen was a nightmare of its own. Dirty dishes towered precariously on the sink, encrusted with mouldy food remnants and swarmed by flies without high standards. The counters were also barely visible beneath piles of crusty pots, pans, and utensils, all coated in a greasy film. The fridge door was ajar, revealing a grotesque scene of spoiled food, covered in a thick layer of mildew and emitting a foul, sour odour.

The bathroom was perhaps the most revolting area of all. The toilet bowl was stained and reeked of ammonia, with the seat covered in further dark, suspicious stains. 'Sit and shit. Don't stand and aim' came to mind. The sink was clogged, and filled with murky, stagnant water. There was a mirror above it smeared with grime. The shower curtain was mouldy and holding on by half of its normal number of rings. It barely covered the tiles which were slick with a grimy residue that made the whole room feel damp and oppressive.

Everything in my body was screaming to leave, but there must be something, anything here that would lead me to the wolf, as everywhere you looked, there were signs of its presence. Tufts of fur clung to furniture and drifted like snowy tumbleweeds across the floor. Scratch marks marred almost all the doors and walls, and a few scattered bones chewed to splintered fragments lay forgotten in corners.

Lastly, I surveyed the bedroom and found the bed was as unmade as I expected, as no one living in filth bothered with fitted sheets. It was a tangled mess of blankets and a stained duvet that was worn thin. Piles of dirty laundry cover the floor, interspersed with wolf fur and remnants of shredded toys. The wardrobe doors hung open, revealing a jumble of clothes, many crumpled and unwashed. He seemed to have worn everything he'd ever owned at one point or another, and then just discarded it in every direction but the washing machine. I prodded at the newest bundles of clothing to see if something was amiss. My unconscious mind was telling me to look there as it must've caught something that needed checking into. The purple purse glinted underneath a pair of grimy jogging bottoms making it look out of place in the mess. It stood out so I gingerly picked it up with a glove I had pulled out of my pocket. There were clear blood stains across the face of the purse.

Opening it, I found the debit card of Mia Simpson.

## Chapter Sixty Eight

### Frustration and devastation

### Jack and Vikki

I don't know why I did what I did next. It was out of character. It wasn't the controlled me I'd always been. There was an urge to go outside, cross the street and leave this building. Was I having a panic attack? I'd never had one before but with everything that had happened to me, around me, had I broken finally? It felt instinctual to the point that I was losing my grip on my bodily movement. Turning, I walked out, handing the evidence to a local officer, and telling him to book it in. I felt my arms removing the gloves I was wearing to cover myself from fingerprinting all the evidence we found and dropped them on the floor. Where was I being taken? I know gazes followed me leave but I seemed unable to control my actions. I was being pulled. Impulsed to leave this building. I felt stairs under my feet as I left, heavy and thudding as if I wasn't thinking about each step. A muffled voice to my side appeared but I couldn't make it out, the words blending into a murmuring mass of sound.

I had to be outside... Under the moon.

*** 

Vikki watched as Jack turned and left the room, the glint of investigation lost in his eyes. She briefly worried for him as if something inside of him had finally broken, which would be perfectly, and terribly, understandable. He seemed drone-like, an autonomous version of the man she had grown to love. Following, she matched his steps down and out of the building. All her asks, her questions were left unanswered and again, she thought that Jack had broken, somewhere deep inside. She'd never seen him like this. He was always aware of everything, never missing anything. The night sky was a blessed relief from the stench of Nathan's home, and she took in lungfuls of cleaner air, although the smell of the room lingered. Jack continued walking, not stopping for anything, and stepped onto the road.

\* \* \*

I knew I was in the street now as the temperature was different, the air sweeter now than it had moments before. I kept walking towards something, wanting, needing to be near whatever was drawing me to its side. I didn't know why, but it was all that mattered. A screeching of tyres filled my ears but still, I continued. Shouts followed and I almost made out one of the voices, it was a female, and she seemed to be bellowing out a warning of some kind.

Still, I continued walking.

\* \* \*

The car had barely missed them both, but Vikki's quick reactions had brought it to an abrupt stop a metre away from the mind-controlled Jack who was still walking towards she knew not what. Jack walked into the darkness of the alleyway across the street and Vikki almost screamed out as she saw the silver-filled eyes of a massive black wolf in front of her.

# Chapter Sixty Nine

## Reunited in the blackness

### Jack

I snapped back to reality and found Vikki and I standing in a dark alley. In front of us was a massive black wolf, similar in size to the white one we were hunting, but this one seemed larger in stature, even as its dark coat blended seamlessly with the night, making it appear even more imposing.

I felt no threat. Immediately I reassured Vikki who while still scared, placed her trust in me. It had all become clear now. My life was leading to this after being bitten all those years ago. I had blocked it from my mind as it came with memories of my dad's murder at the teeth of the grey one.

This was my wolf. He was a part of me as Nathan was part of the white. We were safe because this werewolf was born from my justice-driven mind. It was the good wolf, from 2022. I reached out and placed my hand atop the wolf's head, and the large beast lowered its head as a mark of acceptance. It was incredibly soft which shocked me at first as I would've thought it to be coarse, due to the outside wild living. Standing a few steps behind me, Vikki was watching with wide eyes, her breath catching in her throat. She had heard the stories of wolf companions and werewolves as had I and until now, I thought that they were the words of the insane Nathan. Everything Nathan said made sense now. I felt whole. All parts of me were here now, and Vikki was very much one of them. I glanced back at Vikki, noticing her apprehension.

"It's alright," I said softly, trying to keep my voice calm and reassuring. "This is my wolf. He's been with me for years; I just haven't been open enough to see him. Maybe you helped me see, but there's nothing to be afraid of."

\*\*\*

Vikki took a tentative step forward, her eyes never leaving the wolf. Black turned his head towards her, his gaze steady and unblinking. For a moment, Vikki felt a shiver of fear, but then she noticed the way Black's body language mirrored Jack's calm demeanour.

"Go on," Jack encouraged. "He won't hurt you. I don't know how I know, but his name is Black." Swallowing her fear, Vikki extended a hand slowly, her fingers trembling slightly. The large wolf sniffed her hand, his wet nose cold against her skin. Then, much to her surprise, he nudged her hand with his head, a gentle gesture that seemed almost affectionate, and she let out a breath she didn't realise she'd been holding.

"See?" Jack said with a smile. "He's clearly a good judge of character." Vikki managed a small smile in return, feeling a sense of awe and respect for the detective and their unusual companion.

"I can see that," she replied, her voice steadying. "He's incredible." Jack nodded; his hand still buried in Black's fur.

"Yeah, he is. And I think he can help track the white wolf. But we cannot let any of the others know. If they kill him, I might die too as Nathan said."

## Chapter Seventy

### On a dark, dark night...

### Jack

We had stealthed our way to the doors of the old, crumbling greengrocer's shop, and I narrowed my eyes to try and see into the darkened interior. At my side, Black appeared and motioned within, his eyesight far keener than mine. It was the first time that I noticed that his eyes were purely silver and flowing with a metallic grace. There was no iris or anything you would normally expect, and how he saw was lost on me. Although at this point it was a minor detail. The chaotic nature of this situation would no doubt send me directly to therapy once we had an outcome. All I could think of was stopping Nathan, his wolf, and saving more lives though.

Saving my Vikki.

The building's decrepit state mirrored the decay of Nathan's flat, but we all sensed the possible danger lurking within. Knowing Black was here though helped, as I hadn't a clue what we were going to do when we found the white wolf. Nathan, I could handle him with ease I surmised, but the wolf? Not so much as my shoulder reminded me.

"He's here," I said. Black growled, his tone low and threatening. It still sent shivers down my spine, even though I knew he was on my side. Vikki's grip tightened on her torch, and I glanced at her, not wanting her here, and needing her safely far, far away. She was the woman I loved, and I needed her safe. I opened my mouth to ask, to order her to leave but she returned my look with a determined nod, her eyes reflecting the same resolve that had brought us together in this deadly pursuit. She was still a police officer at heart as I was, and this was our duty.

"Stay close," I whispered, my voice barely audible over the creaking of the old building. "Nathan won't go down without a fight, and his wolf is just as dangerous."

Vikki nodded again, her hand sweeping the torch beam through the dark, dilapidated shop. Black thankfully led the way, his powerful frame moving with a predatory grace that belied his size. He paused occasionally, sniffing the air and listening intently. Vikki and I followed, pausing only to pick up whatever we could find as a weapon. I chose a large board with various rusty nails in it and she picked up a discarded screwdriver. All our senses were heightened to the maximum, as every sound and shadow was a potential threat. As we moved deeper into the shop, we saw that it had been used as a squat for the homeless who were now scattered, literally in some instances around the store.

"White has killed more people than we thought." was all I said, but I hadn't needed to, it was abundantly clear. There were at least two torsos in the shop that were devoid of appendages. I felt anger rise in me that we hadn't caught this monster earlier. But then, how could we have? It was from a nightmare, no one would think that there was a killer with a pet wolf he had birthed from his own body stalking Epsom and killing at their whims.

How many more...?

The remnants of the shop's former life surrounded us. Rotten vegetables lay in heaps, their stench mingling with the musty odour of death and decay. Broken shelves and overturned crates created a labyrinth of obstacles, and my heart pounded in my chest as I navigated the narrow path Black had chosen. Black and I heard a noise echoing from the back of the shop—a faint scuffle, the scrape of claws on wood, and I signalled for Vikki to stop, hoping Black would keep his point at the front. We crouched behind an overturned counter, listening.

"That must be them," Vikki whispered, her voice trembling with fear and anticipation. Still with the same strength I'd fallen for.

I peered over the counter, as her torch cast a thin, penetrating beam into the darkness. There, in the shadows, we saw movement. A figure shifting, almost imperceptible, blending with the gloom.

"Nathan," I called out, trying to steady my voice but also commanding so he obeyed. "It's over. Come out and face us."

For a moment, there was silence. Then, a chilling laugh echoed through the shop, a sound that sent chills down my spine. Vikki shifted next to me, wondering what our next step in the impossible situation would be.

"You think you can stop me?" Nathan's voice was filled with contempt and arrogance. "You and your bitch?"

A figure stepped into the light, tall and gaunt, with eyes that burned with a malevolent fire. Nathan's lips curled into a sneer as he regarded the trio before him.

"I knew you weren't whole the moment I met you," Nathan said, his voice dripping with venom. "White wanted to meet your wolf. He wants to kill it, so he can alpha this world." As if on cue, a low growl reverberated through the shop, and from the shadows emerged

White, the massive werewolf with fur snow white with the same silvered eyes that glowed with a cold, calculating intelligence. He moved to stand beside Nathan, his presence an ominous reminder of the deadly bond between beast and beast.

"Go call for armed units, we'll keep him busy," I said quietly to Vikki, hoping that she would, this once, do as I'd asked. She looked at me with contemplating eyes, weighing up her options. With a voice that was steady despite the fear in her eyes, said;

"Don't die. I need you." It wasn't a request, but an order I wanted to follow just as much. Black stepped forward, his fur bristling, a deep growl emanating from his chest. His stance screamed the words 'This ends now,' but without the vocabulary of its human, the posture would have to do. Everything felt primal now, as the challenge between wolves had been offered to his white-furred counterpart. The air was thick with tension as the two werewolves faced off, muscles coiled, ready to spring.

I waited for Vikki to be clear of the shop and faced off against the man I hated more than anything should ever be hated.

# Chapter Seventy One

## Fight

### Jack

With a roar, Black lunged at White, and the two werewolves collided in a flurry of claws and fangs. The force of their clash sent a shockwave through the shop, and I scrambled to stay out of their path while keeping my eyes on Nathan.

The suspect I wanted the most in my career moved with a speed that belied his frail appearance, darting towards me with a knife in his hand. I parried his first thrust, hitting him hard in the ribs with the board I'd picked up earlier. It caught him off balance and he stumbled away. Luckily for him, I'd not put my full power into it as while I wanted to hurt him, I was still an officer and wanted him to face the full force of the law. I wanted everyone to look upon his face and know justice would be served for all.

Deep down, I wanted him to feel the full force of my makeshift weapon. I wanted the rusty nails to rip and shred whatever they found. Not for me, for all the fallen. They deserved vengeance, but I was holding that back.

At least for now.

"You're a fool, Jack," Nathan hissed, trying again to slash at me with the same wild abandon. "You can't win. Let's be kings of this world. We're beyond humanity now!"

"I don't have to win," I grunted back, deflecting another amateurish strike. "I just have to stop you. Either that or Black will." The thought of the second option brought a smile to my lips.

A yelp of pain brought a wave of pain racking through my body. It echoed through the shop, and I caught sight of Black faltering, blood matting his dark fur. White pressed his advantage, his fangs bared in a savage grin. How I couldn't comprehend, but I realised that I was feeling the wounds as Black did. It was enough to push my guard down. Nathan was on me, his knife buried hilt deep in my leg.

A second yelp of pain from Black, who fell back on his injured flank leg. I screamed in pain as a wave of agony clawed through me, but this time, I fought against the agony that would force unconsciousness. It wouldn't, couldn't take me because if it did, we'd both be dead and Nathan would be free. As the adrenaline of the fight coursed through me. I was now faced with both Nathan and his wolf as they pressed their advantage.

It was at that moment, that briefest of seconds, that I knew my life was ending.

# Chapter Seventy Two

## "Urgent, Active Message!"

### Vikki

From outside, Vikki heard the raised voices and a clamour that made her entire being scream to run back inside. She burned to help Jack, but they needed the reinforcements that would bring the entirety of the police family rushing to their aid.

"Surrey Control. Urgent active message. We found the wolf and need urgent assistance at our location. Requesting armed response units as we have located the wolf." Taking a deep breath, she continued, this time, with the details the teams needed including location, access, and rendezvous points to help the incoming wave of blue.

Only when she finished did her breathing return to normal as units of all types barked in their callsigns, acknowledging that they were on their way. The list was extensive thankfully and Vikki held back the emotions it brought up.

They were coming.

Help was on its way...

Callsigns ended and the incident was declared as critical. Channels were split so that normal business could be kept up, although luckily, there was little of note happening. This was all that consumed the teams. A drunk in the town centre was managed by local safer neighbourhoods Police Community Support Officers who were stepping up to take anything they could to free up more officers.

Vikki's fingers danced over her phone, issuing precise commands to the emergency response team as her heart pounded, her voice remained steady on the radio, ensuring that backup units converged on their precise location.

She clutched at her chest as her heart ached a thumping beat. She continued to frantically coordinate the rescue effort, her voice steady over the radio despite the turmoil inside. She'd just heard a yelp of pain that could have only come from either wolf. She hoped that it wasn't Black and that he was winning out. She barked out orders for reinforcements, medics, and specialists to converge on their location, each word a desperate attempt to save the one she loved.

All she wanted was to be by Jack's side, to fight alongside him against the terrifying werewolf that threatened his life. Every fibre of her yearned to rush to him, to shield him from harm, but she knew her duty was to ensure the right help arrived. As she dispatched the final call for backup, her eyes darted back towards the dilapidated shop, her silent prayer mingling with the wail of approaching sirens.

As the first red and blue lights appeared, she turned and disappeared back inside.

# Chapter Seventy Three

## Death comes a-knockin

### Jack

This was it.

This is how I die.

Not old and grey with Vikki snuggled alongside me. Not watching our grandkids play in our garden. Not with our kids telling us it'll be ok, and it was alright to let go.

I was to be torn apart by a giant fucking wolf while being beaten to death by a sadist.

As I stood there, injured by a stab wound and a bite that felt ethereal, the chilling presence of death crept closer with each passing breath. My body felt heavy, and tired, like it was being pulled down by an unseen force, and a cold numbness spread through my limbs. I hoped it would be fast. The room around me blurred, and in this haze, I couldn't help but think of the one I loved, and all the unknown people I promised to help. Those that should be both protected and served. A deep, gnawing guilt twisted within me, as I felt that I'd let them all down. There were dreams unfulfilled, promises half-kept, and words left unsaid. The weight of my unspoken apology to residents that I wasn't going to be able to help them was all-consuming. These unfinished good deeds bore down on me harder than the darkness encroaching.

In these final moments, the regret was almost as suffocating as the impending end.

On top of this, I had to listen to a gloating monologue from this barbarous killer in front of me.

"So White... Which one to kill? Wanna eat this piggie bastard, or try the wolf? You can only pick one remember as when one dies, they both do. We're still one at heart." His voice was filled with a self-congratulatory tone that made everything he said feel worse. I just wanted it to end now, as I was done with being made to listen to this arsehole anymore.

"Just do it. Kill me. Units are on their way and the armed officers are going to pin cushion you into oblivion." I tasted blood in my mouth so defiantly, I spat it on the floor in front of him.

Movement, off to my left.

It was behind the approaching pair, so I was sure that they hadn't noticed it. It was Vikki. She was creeping up behind them, the large screwdriver held firmly in her grasp. For some unearthly reason, I wondered if it was a flat head or a Phillips, reckoning that I was losing consciousness. The pain was all that was keeping me standing at this point, so my mind was focussing on the trivial.

I wanted her to run back, but knew if I motioned to her anything at this point it would mean her death.

Keep Nathan talking...

"Tell me one thing. How did the wolves begin?"

Nathan knew he had won and liked the sound of his own voice, so I bargained that this would give Vikki and the troops time to get into position.

"It all began when the first cursed wolf started biting the unfortunate. It was revenge for killing her master. She wanted to curse humanity. For a while, they spread as more and more Weres were born, but they were hunted to almost extinction, even though we are a dominant race."

He smiled, licking his lips at his recall.

Vikki inched closer.

"The few that were left went into hiding, only biting when absolutely necessary. Some of these bitten hosts panicked when a giant fucking wolf appeared beside them and that got them killed by their own offspring. Some, the good ones like you, might never even know you had one. You see, the wolves all had this inherent hatred of the humans, as they were hunted years gone. Now though, they know that humans are filth and fodder if trained right. They need to be coaxed out of their shells. Like White here… My stone-cold killer." Nathan patted him on the head affectionately, as Vikki moved a metre closer.

"That's a lovely story you've found on some arsehole conspiracy dark website, but you want to know what I think?" I tried to muster all my strength to stand, using the wooden board as a makeshift crutch.

Nathan was beaming and moving closer, the wolf remaining still.

"Go on then copper. Tell me. Not that it matters now."

He wasn't wrong. If whatever Vikki was planning failed, life was done.

"You're just a sad little man who found power hiding behind a wolf and a fairytale. I pity you."

White snarled.

Vikki plunged the screwdriver to its hilt, through the silver eye of the white wolf.

## Chapter Seventy Four

### If we were one...

### Jack

Nathan was facing me when it happened. He was close and planning to end my life. He had already concluded that he'd won.

Vikki had made it all the way to White's side, such was their complacency. I knew she had something planned but this was not it. What happened after, would stay in my mind till my death.

As the screwdriver was impaled through the silvery orb of the white wolf's eye, Nathan's own exploded outwards in a shower of vitreous fluid and blood. He screamed incredulously at the shock and pain of the impact which had affected the pair in front of me in the same instant. I could see inside Nathan's head where the screwdriver should have been as he clawed at the invisible implement. He tried in vain to remove what had been stabbed into his head, flailing, not fully understanding through the agony. Blood jetted through his fingers and his remaining eye was filled with fear and confusion.

Vikki pushed further, but she realised that she had hit bone, so deep she had plunged it. White was screeching in pain and swung his large head, sending her flying into the debris. She landed with a crash, and I saw she had taken the tool with her, removing it from the gouged socket.

The silver fluid was mixing with the dark red blood creating an ethereal swirl that ran down its snout.

But it wasn't enough.

The white wolf looked at me, then back to Vikki, and was shaking in rage born from violent injury.

It then did what I feared most.

It turned toward Vikki...

...as Black arose.

***

Amongst the debris, chaos ruled. The two wolves began circling each other with a deadly intensity. Both were wounded and all the three humans could do now was watch the final attack.

The wounded black wolf, fur matted with blood and dirt, moved with a determined limp from Jack's knife-wounded leg. His eyes burned with a fierce resolve, as he knew he could end it all with the right attack. His flank bore deep gashes, reminders of a brutal encounter that had left him weakened yet unyielding.

Opposite him stood the white wolf, a beast of stark contrast, with a single eye blazing with a feral, unrestrained rage. The other eye, now a haunting blooded scar, marked him as a creature shaped by violence and vengeance. His growls of violence-laced anger reverberated through the shop, each sound was a promise, a threat, of imminent destruction. His focus, however, was not solely on his onyx adversary but on the woman behind the black wolf – Vikki.

Vikki tried to stand firm behind the black wolf and considered her options as tactfully as fear would allow. Fear raged within her as the white wolf's hatred was palpable, his intention to tear her apart clear in every bristling hair and snarling grimace. He lunged, a blur of white fury and muscle, aiming to bypass the black wolf and reach her.

The black wolf, despite his injuries, surged forward with a primal roar and strength borne from a protective instinct. Their bodies collided in a storm of teeth and claws. Black fought with the ferocity of a guardian; every ounce of his remaining strength channelled into protecting Vikki. He snapped and tore, his teeth sinking into the white wolf's flesh with relentless precision. White, maddened by his ocular loss and driven by a single-minded vendetta, fought back savagely. Blood sprayed and fur flew, the night air filled with the sounds of their brutal clash. Yet, the black wolf's determination was an unbreakable shield. With a final, decisive lunge, he clamped his jaws around the white wolf's throat, his teeth sinking deep until the struggle ceased. The white wolf collapsed, a lifeless heap on the rubbish-littered floor, as Black, breathing heavily, stood over his fallen foe. His eyes were still smouldering with the remnants of battle, as he turned to Vikki, his stance protective yet weary. She stepped forward, her eyes soft with gratitude and sorrow, understanding the depth of the sacrifice made to ensure her safety.

In the quiet aftermath, the black wolf's head bowed slightly, acknowledging both his victory and the toll it had taken. Vikki knelt beside him, her hand gently resting on his fur, a silent vow of companionship and mutual respect binding them in the sudden silence.

\*\*\*

The fight took seconds, and I felt every blow, every bite. But an eerie quiet had fallen in the old shop. We had won. It was over.

The realisation took the last of my strength and I crumpled, landing heavily on the floor. Vikki and Black were then with me, helping and caring. The wolf was licking at the knife wound which was gross and strangely comforting. I raised my hand to pull him closer and I felt whole at that moment. I was complete because he was here and so was Vikki.

I winced as Vikki tied her belt around my leg, to stem the flow of blood pumping from the knife wound. It hurt, but I knew it was standard procedure.

Sitting there, amongst the crap and litter, my breath felt ragged as my whole body ached from the fierce battle. The adrenaline from the fight still coursed through my veins, making my heart pound loudly in my chest. Looking at Vikki, I knew that she was my beacon of strength and resilience, her eyes wide with a mixture of relief and gratitude. I felt my heart swell more, as a torrent of emotions surged through me. Relief washed over me like a warm wave, soothing the raw edges of any fear and anxiety I had left. We had done it; Nathan lay defeated, and Vikki was safe. The weight of the past days' dread lifted from my shoulders, leaving me feeling lighter and almost giddy.

It was more than relief that filled me. Seeing Vikki there, mostly unharmed and looking at me with such profound thankfulness, ignited a fierce, overwhelming love within. It was a love that burst forth, uncontainable and all-encompassing, something I'd never truly allowed myself to feel. My chest felt tight with the intensity of it, my breath caught as I tried to find the right words, and the right actions, to express what I felt.

Nothing seemed enough. No words were worth it.

"I love you."

Vikki looked at me and the tears flowed freely in relief and love. I'd gone from thinking my life was over to being the happiest I'd ever been. I pulled her next to me, my eyes never leaving hers. I just wanted to hold her, to feel the reassurance of her heartbeat against mine, to let her know without words just how much she meant to me. The world around us seemed to fade away again, leaving just the two of us in this moment of shared triumph and deep, abiding affection.

"Vikki," I breathed, my voice thick with emotion. "We did it. You're safe."

Reaching out, I saw that my hand was trembling slightly as it touched her arm, then slid up to cup her face gently. The connection, the sheer warmth of her skin against mine, sent a shiver down my spine. My thumb brushed her cheek, and I drank in every detail of her face as if memorising it anew.

"I was so afraid of losing you," I admitted, my voice barely above a whisper. "But you're here, and I... I love you, Vikki. More than words could ever say."

As I spoke, a tear of relief and joy slipped down my cheek, as the rawness of the moment left me vulnerable yet profoundly alive. The fierce battle had been won, but it was this, the sight of her safe and within reach, that truly made my heart soar.

The body of the White wolf dissolved in front of our eyes. In seconds, all that confirmed it had even been there was a pool of liquid, that shimmered in the flashing lights of the police cars that were arriving on scene.

Nathan was still there though, with a haunted, terrified look on his face. It was like he knew what had happened, even though the death blow happened to his other side. His neck bore heavy bruising and was crumpled in places as if it had been stood on by a heavy-footed assailant.

Blue and red lights continued to flood the rooms, so we decided to go and get medical assistance for our various wounds. Plus, we needed to let our family know that the white wolf would not hurt any more of our people.

I'd never seen so many officers. Dog section, armed response, literally every rank could be seen.

The ambulance was nestled at the back, so we aimed for that as the first gunshot rang out.

# Chapter Seventy Five

## A month later...

## Vikki

It still hurts.

I still saw the muzzle flash.

I still saw the bullets tear into the black wolf.

I remember the feeling of Jack's body going limp as the two connected halves died. I'd been off work since I lost my Jack. Hearing my name and title, 'Detective Vikki Doherty' made me feel physically ill.

My world felt as though it had shattered and stitched itself together in the most agonisingly beautiful yet cruel way. The loss of one so loved brought darkness so profound. It was as if the very essence of my life had been sucked out of the air, leaving everything feeling empty and hollow. Grief hit me like a tidal wave, crashing over every thought and emotion. I was left with a sense of numbness and an aching void that nothing seemed able to fill.

Memories of my Jack flooded my mind, and while we were only together briefly, it had been perfect, even through the chaos. Each thought was now a bittersweet reminder of what had been lost. Our laughter, our touch, the way we looked at each other. How he felt inside. All were now fragments of a past that I could never reclaim. My heartache was a constant, physical pain, an unending reminder of the absence that had suddenly become so palpable. Every corner of my house, every familiar scent, every whisper of the wind seemed to carry echoes of the person who was no longer there.

My Jack.

Then, amid my overwhelming sorrow, came the revelation—unexpected and life-altering. The discovery of my pregnancy brought with it a whirlwind of emotions, crashing through the haze of grief like a beam of light breaking through storm clouds. Shock and disbelief mingled with my sadness, creating a complex tapestry of feelings that were difficult to untangle.

I would sit hugging myself for hours.

The knowledge of a new life growing inside brought a fragile sense of hope and purpose. It was a beacon in the darkness, a reason to hold on and move forward despite the crippling weight of loss. The thought of a piece of Jack living within me was a huge comfort and a source of profound sadness. Our child would never know his or her father, but I would make sure that they would. They had lost without even knowing. The thought that they would never hear his voice or feel his embrace was a fresh wound on top of my already bleeding heart.

"I will always miss you Jack," I would say daily.

Yet, amidst the grief, there was a flicker of joy, a tiny spark of anticipation and love for the unborn child. My future, though shrouded in uncertainty and tinged with sorrow, held the promise of new beginnings. Our pregnancy became a precious connection to Jack, a living testament to the bond we shared. It was a reminder that life, in all its relentless cycles of loss and renewal, continued.

I adopted his cat, Cat. He too seemed to feel the loss of his previous owner in the way cats do. He took to sleeping on my lap, holding my stomach as it grew by the day.

Leigh and I became close in grief and new life. As soon as I found out that I was pregnant, she said that she would stand by me and help raise my child and weirdly, it felt right. We'd always been close, but now, knowing she and I had shared Jack for that one night, made me want to stay with her. We had a deeper connection now.

My emotions were a chaotic blend of grief, hope, despair, and love. Each day was a struggle, a balancing act between mourning the past and nurturing the future. Leigh came into her own and was my rock as the pain of loss was ever-present, but so too was the delicate joy of impending motherhood. It was my journey of resilience and strength, an experience that reshaped my very core of existence, intertwining sorrow with the faint but persistent glow of new life.

It was a life that would reshape our world.

# Epilogue One

## Humanity Falls...

Sky News Report: 27th October 2024

Reporter: Sarah-Jane Mee

18:00 hrs

### Breaking News: Baby Born with Unexplained Aberrational Anomaly Stuns Medical Community

In a remarkable and unprecedented medical event, a baby has been born with a fantastical aberrational anomaly that has left doctors and scientists across the globe bewildered. The newborn, delivered yesterday at St. Mary's Hospital in London, exhibits features that defy all known biological principles.

The baby, named Kay by her parents, Victoria Doherty and partner Leigh Taylor, was born with what appears to be a luminescent, shimmering skin over her back that changes colour in response to various stimuli. This extraordinary characteristic was noticed immediately after birth, as the delivery room was reportedly bathed in an ethereal glow.

Dr Emily Carter, the lead obstetrician present during the birth, described the moment as "utterly surreal." She stated, "In all my years of practice, I have never encountered anything like this. Kay's skin emits a soft, glowing light that varies in hue from blue to pink to gold. It is completely unprecedented in medical history."

The hospital has since called in experts from various fields, including geneticists, biologists, and physicists, to understand the underlying cause of this anomaly. Despite extensive testing and analysis, no clear explanation has emerged. Preliminary genetic tests have shown no known mutations or abnormalities that could account for the luminescence.

Dr Michael Turner, a leading geneticist from the University of Oxford, expressed his astonishment: "This is a phenomenon that goes beyond our current understanding of human biology. The mechanisms that could produce such an effect are not present in any known genetic or biochemical pathways. We are truly in uncharted territory."

Kay's parents, while initially shocked, are embracing the uniqueness of their daughter. "She is our little miracle," said Victoria Doherty. "We are in awe of her and just want to make sure she is healthy and happy. We hope that as more is understood about her condition, it will help illuminate new areas of science. It might be hard, but if a job's worth doing, it's worth doing right."

The medical community is now urging other hospitals to report any similar cases, hoping to find more data that could lead to an understanding of Kay's condition. In the meantime, she is being closely monitored, and her health appears to be normal aside from her extraordinary appearance.

As news of Kay's birth spreads, it has captivated the public imagination, with social media abuzz with speculation and wonder. Some have even begun to refer to her as the "Luminescent Child," symbolising hope and mystery, whilst others have expressed concern about the risk to the general public.

Sky News will continue to follow this developing story, bringing you the latest updates as the medical investigation progresses. For now, Kay remains a shining beacon of the unknown, a living reminder of the mysteries that still lie within the human genome.

Her father was not available for comment.

## Epilogue Two

## Darkness Rises...

## Chapter one

### 1692

Plymouth.

What an accursed name. The inbred denizens of the new town couldn't even bring themselves to craft a new name, having copied it from the port town in Britain from whence they came.

Plymouth was one of the earliest settlements established by English colonists in America, the New World as everyone was told. It was founded by the Pilgrims, a group of Separatists who sought religious freedom from the Church of England. It was founded in 1620 when the Pilgrims aboard the Mayflower arrived, quickly establishing the Plymouth Colony.

They wanted true freedom.

She too wanted a taste of freedom, but she had to leave for other reasons. This wasn't a new start for her. It was just time to move on because they were getting too close to finding out her secrets. She joined the boat with the pilgrims, hiding in their very midst. Their God would've hated her being on the same ship, hated that she was eating at the same table as their leaders. The Pilgrims were a tight-knit religious community with strong beliefs and values, seeking to create a society based on their interpretation of Christianity, emphasising principles of hard work, self-reliance, and communal cooperation.

How wrong they were to be. They were blind to what was hiding in plain sight among them because she was used to hiding. She hid everything well. The large case was one she especially wanted to be hidden away. It was on the lowest of decks after a bribed deckhand sneaked it aboard. It had all her worldly possessions hidden inside it.

'Worldly…' she smiled broadly at the word, showing yellowed teeth to those who caught sight of her. Each night she would venture into the hold and feed the precious contents, sustaining her beloved half.

Sarah and her mysterious cargo settled on the outskirts of Salem village, a small farming town where the inhabitants loved to argue about everything. She craved that, because while they disputed grazing rights, property lines, or anything that they could bicker about she hid in their shadows. She managed to get by on what she could forage, or steal, such was her stealth. She had a secret to keep. She had her wolf to love. The large beast was called Bruna, a large brown wolf, oversized by her kin. She had been with her as a loyal servant and protector for as long as she could remember. It was born from her, and they'd felt as one as soon as they had met. This new land was perfect for Bruna.

She flourished.

The woodland nearby held a variety of creatures to hunt and kill in the night. She'd even picked off a few of the local indigenous population and caused them to leave the area, thinking it cursed, or even evil. Feuds between families broke out, with allegiances tested between them as they fought over quarrelsome borders or trades. Life in Plymouth was harsh and challenging, especially during the early years, as the settlers faced food shortages, harsh weather, and disease, which took a toll on their population. The problems worsened when the local villagers wanted their church in town. 1689 brought Samuel Paris and he was a Puritan wholeheartedly. He would punish people for minor infractions, almost always involving some sort of public humiliation. Even the villagers hated him, going as far as to remove his access to firewood.

The priesthood grew in power with each year, and Sarah had to withdraw further inward, away from this zealot-filled urban district. Paris would fill his sermons with tales of devils and demons, witches and spreading evil. He'd seen the growing of the darkness.

Refugees fled to both Salem and Salem village, fleeing the war that was raging. They weren't made welcome as they stretched the resources in an already tense village where no one had lived happily for years.

During the year 1692, under their lord, the real pain began.

## Chapter Two

Paris' daughters, nine and eleven, fell ill simultaneously, throwing both fits and items as they contorted themselves into strange positions. They would screech at all hours, claiming to see visions, nightmares, and hallucinations through feverish nights. Sarah thought this would finally rid her village of the evil zealot Paris. The children would not be hurt, she wasn't a monster.

She tried to scare the family just enough so that they would leave, never to return. A doctor called in and he claimed that the children were somehow possessed and worse still, that it was contagious.

The idiot.

Sarah had simply added some select herbs and berries to the children's water supply to force them into their current state. Unfortunately, other children claimed to have the same fits, which convinced the village that there was a curse upon them.

Cries of 'Devils' and 'Witches' filled the streets and Sarah was locked up with two other women. The incarceration was torture in all senses of the word.

Bruna was left alone and came to the barred window of the small court lock room each night. She'd chew at the bars, trying to get Sarah free. They were lost without each other.

After a week of questioning in which magistrates would bully, injure, and look for any kind of evidence to break the other two women, finally they both relented and confessed to being witches.

The investigations were ridiculous. The male

magistrates would search the naked females for blemishes or marks where the devil had drunk their blood in exchange for their new ungodly ensorcelled powers.

They weren't ready for the mark on Sarah's body.

All withdrew from the sight of the foot-long scar along Sarah's back where Bruna had emerged.

She was not a witch.

She was something far worse.

\*\*\*

Sarah Osbourne had felt something was changing deep within her in Lancashire years prior and fell into the Weresleep that same night. She remembered nothing of the change but had felt everything.

The ripping and tearing of old flesh.

The feeling of fur pushing itself out of her body.

Bruna was born that night. She was a brown Wulf, larger than a standard wild Wulf. She had a muscular frame covered in thick, coarse fur, a deep shade of brown that blended seamlessly with the shadows of the night.

The fur was matted in some places, covered in the blood of its former host. It sat cleaning and bathing itself while her mother regained consciousness. Sarah healed as she slept, the gaping rip along her spine sealing itself once more. The birth was exhausting, but as she blinked her eyes, she somehow knew that she was safe.

She had become the first of the Wulf bloodline, and it would mix the male Weres and female Wifs. As the silver otherworldly orbs looked back at her host, her mother, the young Wulf knew that she was not to devour this wounded, fragile body, even though the scent of blood was heavy in the air.

Bruna twitched her sharp, pointed ears which protruded from her shaggy mane, twitching at every sound. They were keenly attuned to their surroundings and moved closer to her mother on the bed. The bedclothes were soaked with the blood of the transformation and Bruna lapped gently at the scar, now sealed as if done in years past. It was an affectionate lick, one of nursing, of care. Bruna's eyes gleamed with both intelligence and ferocity, born of its resilient mother, showing both halves primal survival instincts which were tempered by a semblance of cunning. Massive claws extended from its paws, capable of rending flesh and bone with ease, while its teeth, elongated and razor-sharp, were barred when ready to attack.

The Wulf lay down on the bed and it creaked under the beast's weight. Nuzzling next to her mother, both host and beast fell asleep. Beneath the beastly exterior lay half a human soul, forever trapped between the worlds of woman and Wulf. They would look after each other, for as long as the years allowed them, hiding in the shadows if they must, fighting, fleeing, if they were able.

## Chapter Three

The scar was all the magistrates needed, as panic and hysteria spread like wildfire. Opportunistic families took full advantage of this and claimed their foes were also witches, causing a multitude of further arrests. All the opponents of grazing rights and property boundaries were locked up, filling the cells. A court was born specifically to convict the witches. A sixty-year-old woman was first, the town gossip who liked a roll in the hay. Married three times, her reputation was the exact opposite of the town's puritanical views.

She was the perfect witch.

Damning evidence from enthusiastic witnesses spewed forth testimony that they had heard the woman screaming about her hatred of God and her love of the Devil. Even a cat was claimed to be bewitched. A guilty verdict brought the hangman's noose. Mass hysteria caused five more deaths, and the public was baying for blood.

Sarah was dragged before the court in August 1692.

\* \* \*

The summer was in full bloom and the heat was dry. The crowd had amassed in front of the gallows, their shouts clamouring for the death of the witch. The quiet town of Salem, where whispers of witchcraft danced on the winds and fear coiled around every corner, became the place where so many had died. So many had been murdered on hearsay.

Sarah was dragged in front of them in chains and rags, her feet scraping the rough stones scattered around the street floor. She was filthy from her enforced incarceration. Frantically, she looked for Bruna who was hidden in the tree line, waiting for a signal.

None would come.

Sarah made eye contact and, at that moment, told her Wulf to stay in the shadows. Stay in them forever, so that she would live, while she was hung. Tears began streaming down her face as the inevitable events played out. The voices of the crowd and the magistrate numbed her senses. So she blocked them out to hear them no more.

As the coarse rope was placed over her neck, it was pulled taut, almost stopping the air before the imminent hanging. Sarah begged whoever would listen to spare Bruna from dying, to let at least half of her be free.

Sarah looked out at the crowd as the last rites were shouted judiciously out to all that gathered. The sermon was filled with baited warnings of still more witches among them all and they should report whoever they knew to be wicked. The magistrate warned all should repent the evil among them and angry glances flicked from person to person.

A rotten tomato streaked past Sarah's head, narrowly missing everyone on the platform. The overly ripe fruit impacted with a squelch behind the gallows, but her attention was on one in the crowd ahead. She had a wild mane of raven hair and eyes that seemed to hold the secrets of the universe. She was standing in silence among a mob baying for blood, with a hood hung around her shoulders. It flowed into a dark cloak which was surprisingly unmarked by the filth of the streets they all walked. It was a rich satin material, with an expensive-looking hem around the cloak's edge. It gave her a look that was clearly out of place to the villagers around her, but none took any notice of her presence.

As if she was not among the thronged mass at all. As accusations flew like arrows through the air, Sarah watched this woman. She was entranced and all thoughts of her inevitable death were gone.

Somehow, she was at peace.

The trial had been swift and merciless, conducted in the shadow of suspicion and fuelled by the flames of paranoia. Testimonies were twisted, evidence was fabricated, and reason gave way to superstition. Sarah had stood before the court, her heart heavy with the weight of injustice, as the verdict was pronounced: guilty.

Nothing mattered anymore.

She felt not fear, but a strange sense of peace. The woman in the crowd seemed to float on ethereal air up to her, her presence unseen by all eyes around.

"I heard your call. Become part of me. If we were one, we'd have all we need to torment these cattle to extinction. Join with Nyx-tryn, goddess of malice and feel powers untold."

Sarah closed her eyes, embracing the stillness that enveloped her, and heard whispered words of solace to the spirits of the dead, and looked to Bruna. She freed her from the constraints of their connection, allowing her to be free to flee.

As the trapdoor fell away beneath her feet, Sarah felt herself lifted from the earth, her spirit soaring free from the shackles of mortality. In that moment, she became more than a woman condemned; she became a symbol of resilience, a beacon of vengeance in the darkness of ignorance and fear.

It was at that moment, that briefest of seconds, that she felt her life end.

A new one was born. One of vengeance. One of malice.

As she drifted away, she cursed the bloodline of the magistrate. Her murderer. His bloodline would know fear, would know chaos, would know pain.

But her anger and pain grew as she drifted. Her curse spread throughout the massed congregation. Sarah watched as it licked beneath them, unseen by their hate filled eyes, but she saw it. It crept from person to person, touching each in different ways, but cursing them all still.

Bruna turned and ran into the dark forest.

With that, the bloodline curse spread like a ravenous virus, leaving no one untouched.

## Appendix

### Trigger Warning details

This book is a complete work of fiction but contains details that some readers may find difficult or uncomfortable, which include;

Suicide

Mental health issues - stress and PTSD

Non consensual sex

A missing girl

Various gruesome deaths

Some scenes of a sexual nature

The death of a child

Pet death

If you need any help or support with any of the issues raised, please reach out and talk to someone.

Help is there for everyone who needs it.

www.ingramcontent.com/pod-product-compliance
Lightning Source LLC
Chambersburg PA
CBHW010817250626
47156CB00011B/3108